The Book of Sauces

By *C. Herman Senn*

Author of "Practical Gastronomy", "The
Twentieth Century Cookery Book", etc.

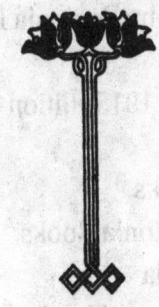

Creative Cookbooks
Monterey, California

The Book of Sauces

by
C. Herman Senn

ISBN: 1-58963-914-6

Copyright © 2002 by Fredonia Books

Reprinted from the 1915 edition

Creative Cookbooks
An Imprint of Fredonia Books
Monterey, California
http://www.creativecookbooks.com

In order to make original editions of historical works available to scholars at an economical price, this facsimile of the original edition of 1915 is reproduced from the best available copy and has been digitally enhanced to improve legibility, but the text remains unaltered to retain historical authenticity.

PREFACE

Since sauces accompany practically every dish, whether it be savory (fish or meat) or a sweet, it follows that sauce-making constitutes a most important branch in cookery. An apology is therefore nardly needed for the publication of a volume devoted entirely to the art of preparing sauces.

It was, I believe, the great maître-chef Câreme who put a premium on any original creation in cookery. To him it mattered little if people criticised adversely new dishes which he introduced. He had such confidence in his ability to create something artistic as well as original that he could afford to wait while his rivals endeavored to spoil the reputation of his Hollandaise or Salmis. Today an innovation in cookery is subjected to practically the same fire of criticism. One season it is the introduction of a new Entrée or Hors-d'oeuvre, the next the culinary worl sits in judgment on a certain sauce which becomes fashionable as an adjunct to a famous Entrée or Entremet.

Whilst disclaiming originality of the many standard sauces which are treated in this book, all of which are to be found in most of the complete cookery manuals, a large number of compound and auxiliary sauces combining entirely new creations have been included in this book.

It is hoped that this collection of sauce recipes, which is claimed to be the largest and most complete ever published in one volume, will meet the wants of professional cooks as well as amateurs, and thus fulfill a useful mission. With the exception of standard and stock sauces, the ingredients given with each recipe are based to be sufficient for a full service of six or seven persons.

C. H. S.

THE BOOK OF SAUCES

The History of Sauce Making.

Sauces, according to the famous maîtres, chefs and culinary artists of the past, Carême and Soyer, ''are to cookery what grammer is to language, and melody is to music''; whilst that intellectual causeur, the Marquis de Cussy, goes so far as to call the artist in sauces ''an enlightened chemist—the creative genius of the high-class cuisine.''

When the practice first began of roasting food —particularly meat—on the spit, broiling it on the gridiron, and boiling it in large cauldrons, sauces and gravies did not come into the reckoning as yet, the instinctive desire for them being satisfied instead by various aromatic herbs and saline (from which is derived ''salsa,'' the word from which our ''sauce'' comes) adjuncts to the meal. It is, in fact, only the very choicest morsels of meat, and these only when prepared by the most skilful hands, which, when roasted, fried, or grilled are found savory without sauce, for these contain sufficient juice to prevent them from being dry and insipid. The Englishman even of the present day scorns the sauces of German cookery; but is glad to make the acquaintance of a good French sauce served with roast, baked, or fried meat, or with plain boiled vegetables.

That there is a standing need for liquid adjuncts for food is indisputable. The modern English method furnishes a very good illustration of the way in which the typical sauce, brought to perfection by the French, has passed through various stages to the lofty eminence it now holds. The ancient Greeks and Romans certainly did prepare sauces, but theirs, as certain others of to-day, not only had no methodical relation to the dishes they accompanied, but were often glaringly unsuited thereto. For instance, the following two sauces, one for meat and the other for mushrooms. are recommended by Apicius, the great Roman gastronomer of Tiberius' time. The former is composed of pepper, dried herbs, coriander-seed, rue, fish-brine, honey, and a little oil, all well-ground and thoroughly mixed. For the sauce for mushrooms the ingredients are: oil, thyme, beans, caraway-seeds, salt, pepper, ginger, wine, and a small quantity of the mysterious "sylphium," now thought to be assafœtida. It goes without saying that pungent sauces like these must completely overpower and alter the individual flavor of any kind of food. The cooks of ancient Rome, making a virtue of necessity, needed to vie with each other in giving quite a different taste to the meats they prepared; imparting to pork, for instance, the flavor of partridge; to goose, that of fish; and to tunny, that of veal. This absurd mania reaches its climax in the performance of that French cook who is said to have prepared a delicious ragoût from—a leathern glove! "But the sauce! that is my secret, my work of art, my glory!"

The cooks of the Middle Ages were rather lavish in the use of salt, pepper, and other condiments, much more so than those of antiquity; this is shown by a cookery book by Moutardier-Gilde, published in 1394. Sugar and other sweet substances were also used in abundance by the cooks of that period; and thus the sauces affected then became a heterogeneous mélange which would almost horrify our modern taste. Let us take two or three examples. For roast goose: chief ingredient, milk, stirred over the fire with flour, salt, pepper, saffron, pounded almonds, and goose-dripping; the name of this concoction is given as "goose-milk." Served with roast beef: roasted apples, raisins, pepper, nutmeg, ginger, and sugar and port wine boiled together and strained, the whole forming a kind of sauce called "Probeat." We thus see that the Middle Ages had but little to teach us in our culinary affairs, and especially so far as sauces are concerned.

When the gastronomic reforms begun in all its glory under Catherine de Medicis and Anne of Austria revealed French cookery (the basis of all good international cookery in our own times) it was perceived that the one and only use of a sauce was to heighten the flavor of a special dish. It was Marperger who, in 1718, instituted the use of the word "tunke" in Germany for "sauce proper," to distinguish it more accurately from "gravy," with which the German name "sause" or "sulze" was apt to be confused. Even now the word for sauce in Low German is "tunke" or "stippe," the characteristic of this preparation in some parts of Germany being that it is of a consistency to allow of the people dipping ("tunking" or "stipping") morsels of solid food in it; while in their thin gravy on the other hand, they would let the pieces swim till dissolved, the whole being then drunk as liquor. A correct sauce is that wonderful production of the culinary art which forms so pleasant and exquisite an accompaniment to all kinds of fish, meat, poultry, and game, or vegetables. The onion-flavored cream sauce "Soubise" is said to have been invented by the Lord High Steward the Marquis de Béchamel, whilst history tells us that the brown onion "Sauce Robert" owes its name by being the head cook of King Francis I.

The skill and knowledge of a cook is shown in no other part of the culinary art so prominently than in the way in which his or her sauces are prepared. To be able to make a perfect sauce is indeed the height in the art of cooking.

The most simple dishes can be made relishable by the addition of a good plain sauce, whilst the most recherché dishes can be improved and be made still more palatable by a well-made sauce, just as a good painting is made smarter by being varnished.

Sauces in cookery may be termed the essence of elegance of dishes with which they are served.

Before we enter into the various details of preparation of the compositions of sauces, I am anxious to point out that every sauce, whether plain or rich, must possess a decidedly distinct flavor and character. There are many plain sauces which are made quickly and of materials usually at hand. Let these be as the name implies, simple and pure, so that they may merely taste of the materials employed, from which such sauces take their name.

Richer sauces always require a longer and slower process for their preparation.

Until the beginning of the nineteenth century, the art of sauce making was hardly known in England. The charge made at that time against the English nation by a celebrated epigrammist, who said that we had many religions but only one sauce, would hardly hold good today, for it is reckoned that there are at least 650 different sauces and gravies known at this moment. An ingenious cook will have as little trouble to form that number of sauces in different varieties, as a musician with his seven notes, or a painter with his pallet and colors; nor is it too much to assert that there is no other branch in cookery which offers better opportunities to display the ability of a cook than this.

The art of sauce making consists in preparing liquids from various materials by cleverly extracting and combining certain flavors into the liquid. Besides this the gift of a good palate is essential, which likewise requires all the experience and skill of the most accomplished cook, as well as a thorough knowledge of the taste of those for whom he or she is cooking.

Distinction between Sauces and Gravies: As there are many people who do not know the distinction between sauces and gravies, it is necessary to devote a few words to this subject, so as to make this quite clear. A gravy is not a sauce, but simply the juices of meat (roasted or braised meat) seasoned but without being thickened, whilst a sauce may be defined, using the most general term, as a liquid seasoning containing some kind of liaison or thickening which is employed in the presentation of food.

According to the chief dictionaries, a gravy may be called a sauce, although a sauce is not always a gravy. Many of the ''grande'' sauces contain gravies for their foundation which are used in a concentrated form to enrich the flavor of such sauces. It is therefore more distinctive to call liquids pure and simple gravies, and liquids thickened with flour or other ingredients sauces, such as ''liaisons,'' thickenings or bindings.

Liaisons: The various processes of thickening sauces as well as soups are called liaisons. There are six distinct methods known for thickening sauces:

1. Liaison with roux.
2. Liaison with eggs.
3. Liaison with butter and cream.
4. Liaison with kneaded butter and flour.
5. Liaison with blood.
6. Liaison with cornflour, arrowroot, or fecula.

Roux: The most popular and most generally adopted thickening is effected by means of roux. It is therefore necessary to first give a few details to define the word roux in regard to its culinary meaning.

Literally the word means russet, but in the culinary sense it is a mixture of flour and butter cooked or blended to certain degrees, to white, to brown, or to fawn colors. The quantity of flour and butter employed are used in equal proportions. If made beforehand in large or small quantities, it should be kept in covered jars, when it will keep good for months. A tablespoonful is usually found sufficient to thicken a pint of liquid. Stock-roux must always be kept in a cool place and ready at hand for use.

If used cold it may be mixed with cold or hot stock, but if mixed cold, it must be stirred constantly over the fire until boiling; or if mixed hot, the liquid should be poured by degrees into the roux away from the fire, and then stirred over the fire till it boils.

Special precaution must always be exercised in making a sauce with a roux thickening, that the temperature is lowered, or, in other words, that the roux is allowed to cool a little before the liquid stock or gravy is added. This will prevent the sauce from getting lumpy, and will do much towards making a sauce perfectly smooth. All roux must be stirred constantly during the process of cooking, *i. e.*, frying.

White Roux (Roux Blanc): This is a mixture of flour and water, cooked in a stew-pan, on a moderate fire, without allowing it to attain any color, whereby it should retain its original white color.

Blonde or Fawn Roux (Roux Blond): This is made by melting a certain quantity of butter, and stirring in the same or a less quantity of sifted flour, and by cooking it over a slow fire or in the oven until it has acquired a light blonde or fawn color.

Brown Roux (Roux Brun): This is the so-called Stock-Roux, which can be prepared in large quantities to be used cold as required as before explained.

It is made exactly in the same manner as the foregoing, with the exception that it is fried longer until it becomes a darker color, a chestnut brown, or russet brown. It is best to finish the roux in a slack oven, for the slower the process the better the blending and the finer the aroma of the sauce will subsequently be.

Roux Liaison: This liaison is made by pouring prepared strained stock gradually into the stewpan containing the roux, which, as before explained, must be allowed to cool off a little. The contents is then stirred over a slow fire until it boils, and is then allowed to simmer until it attains the desired consistency. With brown and blonde sauces the roux employed is usually made up with a "mirepoix" to introduce the necessary flavorings. This item "mirepoix" is more fully explained further on.

Egg Liaison: This is a thickening composed of yolks of eggs beaten up and diluted with a small quantity of cream, milk, or cold white stock. Cream is more often used than stock. The sauce to which this liaison is added must necessarily be boiling, it is then removed to the side of the stove, when a ladleful of sauce is stirred into the egg mixture, then the whole is poured into the sauce, and stirred over the fire (slow) for several minutes, without permitting it to boil.

Every sauce or soup which is thickened with eggs should be passed through a tammy before it can be served. This liaison is used largely for blanquettes, white ragoûts, and fricassés as well as for soups.

Butter and Cream Liaisons: Butter and cream are incorporated in equal proportions into sauces and soups, just before they are wanted for serving. Stir vigorously without reheating. The flavor of any sauce would become altered if butter or cream were added too soon, or if a sauce were again allowed to boil. The same may be said of butter liaisons. By this process a quantity of cold fresh butter is added in small bits to sauces the moment they are taken off the fire, they are then stirred with a whisk and served without being reheated.

Kneaded Butter Liaison: Incorporate or knead as much flour into butter as it will absorb to form a soft paste, and to mix it in small portions into a thin sauce (hot), stirring it constantly until all the butter is melted, constitutes what is called a kneaded butter liaison.

Blood Liaison: This is mostly used with hare or other game entrée sauces. It is made by preserving the blood of hare or game, to which is added a little vinegar to prevent it from coagulating; it is then strained through a fine sieve, and stirred gradually into sauces a few minutes before serving. This kind of liaison is but little used now.

Farinaceous Liaisons: Arrowroot, corn-flour, potato-flour, rice flour (fégulæ), or other similar farinaceous preparations are frequently used for thickening sauces. Dilute one or the other of these with a little milk, cold stock, or water, pour it through a strainer into boiling liquid, stir continually until it boils, then simmer gently for ten or fifteen minutes longer.

Mirepoix: Although the word mirepoix is a common term in culinary matters, it does not in the least imply or make clear what it constitutes. It is one of the many words which the gastronomic authorities ought to abolish and substitute with a more appropriate one, one that conveys more clearly the meaning of the composition of the title it bears. History tells us that Mirepoix was a Duke whose wife, being a clever cook, became a favorite with Louis XV. I, however, fail to see what this has to do with this culinary adjunct used in the preparation of sauces and soups, braises, and stews. To come to the point, let me explain that a "mirepoix" is nothing less than an essence or extract of meat and vegetables, one of the most useful preparations to impart flavor of exquisite richness in various kinds of sauces, soups, and other culinary preparations.

To make a mirepoix properly, use the following ingredients: ½ lb. bacon (ham or gammon) cut into small pieces, 1 carrot (slices), 1 or 2 bay-leaves, a sprig of thyme, 2 small onions (sliced), a clove of garlic, 2 shallots.

Fry these carefully without actually browning, and the mirepoix proper will be complete. It will afterwards, according to requirements, be diluted and boiled up with wine, sherry, chablis, sauterne, or claret, which will be added to stock or to sauce to simmer in it and to give it the desired flavor.

Many chefs do not consider a mirepoix complete without a certain quantity of veal or other lean meat, being added. This I maintain to be waste-ful, as the stock employed should contain the necessary flavor of meat needed. The addition of bacon or ham has, on the other hand, quite a different effect as to its flavor, and I cannot speak too highly of it.

Essences of Meat, etc.: Essences or extracts of meat, fish, poultry, and game are largely employed in the various sauce preparations. These are de-coctions or concentrated liquids containing as much as possible of the flavors, which by certain processes are reduced to the consistency of half-glaze.

To make an Essence: The materials from which the essence takes its name are put in a stew-pan with a quantity of rich stock, wine, vegetables, and herb flavoring. When sufficiently simmered the liquor is strained into another stew-pan, and when thoroughly skimmed and freed from fat it is re-duced to the consistency needed and put by for use when required.

The following essences are those most frequently used in high-class kitchens:

Ham essence, truffle essence, fish essence, mush-room essence, chicken essence, rabbit essence, game essence, pheasant, woodcock, snipe, partridge and lark essence, etc.

These essences are, of course, used to enrich certain sauces, so as to make their characteristic flavor more conspicuous. It is needless to add that the use of essences is only adopted for very rich sauces, etc.

Fumet: A fumet is very much the same preparation as essences, but much richer, being reduced with sherry or madeira wine. Fumet, in other words, may be termed the flavor, being in reality the condensed steam which rises from certain cooked and raw meats, game, or poultry, whereby a most exquisite and agreeable flavor is obtained. For a fumet the raw ingredients required are usually sautéed in the first instance, after which a bouquet of herbs, stock, and wine are added for reduction purposes.

Foundation Sauces: All the great sauces, as they are called in France, have either well reduced stock or essences for their foundation. Espagnole, Velouté, Allemande, and Béchamel, are the names of the four sauces known as "les grandes sauces," though the actual leading foundation sauces are a brown and a white sauce.

Espagnole and Béchamel: These are justly termed the Adam and Eve of all their other preparations, because from these an endless variety of sauces can be made.

If we look into the above statement concerning the four grande sauces more closely, we find that Espagnole is a brown sauce, whilst the other three are white sauces. This must strike the uninitiated as somewhat odd, because only one brown sauce is recognized, whereas in cookery a brown sauce is used at least three times as often as a white sauce. It is furthermore curious, or apparently so, to note that the brown sauce which the French cuisine recognizes as *the* sauce should be called Spanish (Espagnole).

The white sauce has two varieties—the Béchamel, and Allemande or Velouté. It would, however, be much more distinctive to recognize but two kinds of sauces as foundation or grande sauces, viz.:

The Espagnole (Spanish) and the Béchamel, which are unquestionably the two leading sauces in cookery, and as such is the case they deserve to receive special recognition.

Sauce Espagnole versus Brown Sauce: There are many people who imagine that Espagnole sauce is nothing more than an ordinary brown sauce. The French cuisine practically owes much of its advancement in cookery to Spain, although the French have excelled the Spanish cuisine by a long way. Spanish cookery was at one time the pioneer, when no doubt this sauce was introduced into France, and such being the case, it cannot be wondered at that the French cooks have stuck to the name of so important a sauce, which they have adopted as their chief brown sauce.

The great secret about this brown sauce consists in the hammy flavor, which is blended into the sauce in such a skilful manner, which makes it superior and distinguishable from an ordinary brown sauce.

Much of the success of a brown sauce—a fundamental sauce—depends upon the manner in which the flour is blended, or, to be more correct, roasted. The principle of roasting flour is practically the same in every instance, although there are a number of ways of introducing the roast flavor into a brown sauce. To illustrate my meaning in this respect, let us take the roasting of coffee as an example, which will give us some idea as to what happens in roasting flour for a sauce. We know that when coffee is properly roasted its aromatic qualities are developed, whereby certain salts and volatile oils are blended, bringing out an excellent aroma, which by mere boiling of the berry could never be attained.

The result obtained by torrefaction is not merely a change of color and an access of fragrance, but also the development of qualities which affect the human frame, which exhilarate the nervous system. The process of roasting flour and the subsequent result in sauces is to a certain extent the same. To roast the flour to a nut-brown color develops a fragrance of the most exquisite flavor, which will ultimately be incorporated into the sauce or sauces.

Time required for cooking: In cooking this as well as other sauces, which require a process of long cooking, it should be remembered that a sauce must simmer long enough to clear and have the fat separated and come to the surface, so that it can be skimmed off.

The introduction of ham, or lean bacon, this being more often used than ham, into the leading brown sauce is but one out of many other ways of incorporating a so-called smoky or hammy flavor, which makes the Espagnole so characteristic, and there is no question as to whether this addition really improves the flavor, for I can assert with every confidence that the best French cooks put ham with due discretion into practically every first-class brown meat sauce or brown meat soup. We do not, therefore, need any further conviction as to the usefulness of ham in brown sauces.

It is well worth noting that although the addition of ham is excellent for brown sauce preparations, the introduction of anything approaching the flavor of ham into white sauces has just the opposite effect, being entirely opposed to its character. This shows at once that the nature of white sauce is produced by blending and ebullition alone, so as to keep it quite free from any of the smoky or incalescent flavors.

Béchamel, Velouté and Other White Sauces: Sauces of this class need not always be essentially white, for very often they are of a creamy, yellow or greenish tint; but the white sauces, the foundation sauces proper, are the result of what has already been explained—viz. a blending of flour and butter, perfected by a certain amount of ebullition, which in the first stage becomes a white coulis, or a velouté, which is subsequently enriched with cream, yolks of eggs, or butter, in order to give it the required distinctive character.

Brown Sauces: The brown sauce, on the other hand, has to go through a process of roasting in the first instance—viz. the preparation of the brown roux, which is roasting flour and butter, to impart the distinctive flavor. This, in addition to the boiling and simmering processes by which the various meats, vegetables, and other ingredients are prepared, produces a brown sauce.

Plain or Simple Sauces: It must be remembered that ordinary sauces, prepared on the quick system, should be allowed to boil at least ten minutes from the time the liquid is added. When a sauce is cooked less than ten minutes.

the flour will not have had time to develop its
full flavor for sauces, and the butter only partially separates, which gives to the sauce a
greasy appearance.

Overcooking of Sauces: It sometimes happens
that by some oversight or error a sauce is
cooked so long that it becomes oily. In this case
a little cold stock, cold milk or water should
be added, and if the sauce is stirred until it
begins to boil it will again become perfectly
smooth, but it must not on any account be
allowed to boil any longer. It must be removed
from the fire immediately before it actually
boils.

Error in Overseasoning: Many a plain sauce
is spoilt by cooks who are too fond of using
spicy flavorings. They seem to me to be unable
to make a sauce without adding one or more
dashes of bottled sauces, spices, etc., thinking
that these additions must necessarily be an improvement. This practice, I need hardly say, is
a much mistaken one, for such additions often
overpower the essential, natural flavor of their
plain sauces, by overloading them with ingredients which are unpalatable. A plain sauce,
as a rule, needs nothing in the way of seasoning,
except salt and pepper, to bring out the flavor
and to stimulate or awaken the palate. Those
who wish for piquancy of flavor will always find
means to satisfy their wants from the cruet.

Characteristic of Sauces and Seasoning: No
matter what the character of a sauce may be,
remember that in all compound sauces, whether
plain or rich, the rule for seasoning and flavoring is the same in every case: that is, the ingredients used for this purpose should be so pro-
portioned that no flavor predominates over the
other, so that by a careful and judicious combination of flavors the sauce or sauces prepared
will not fail to be acceptable to the palate of
the most refined gourmet.

Cook's Duty Regarding Taste: Furthermore,
remember that it is a cook's duty to study the
likes and dislikes as to seasoning and flavoring
of those for whom she or he works, whereby
certain ingredients for every sauce must neces-

sarily be increased or lessened according to taste. If this is done, no one need fail to become master of the art of sauce-making, so far as the extraction and combination of flavors in sauces are concerned.

On the Reduction of Sauces: We reduce or boil down sauces to give them the necessary strength and consistency. This is usually the case with the compounds into which stocks, essences, fumets, etc., have been incorporated: these are added for the express purpose of reduction, and should be in a concentrated form, so as to lessen as much as possible the labor of boiling or simmering. All sauces which need to be reduced must be strained and freed from fat; they must be put on a quick fire at first, and must be stirred with a wooden spatula or spoon to prevent the sauce from adhering to the bottom of the saucepan in which the sauce is put. The necessary quantity of stock, etc., required for its improvement is next added; it is then allowed to boil until it has acquired the desired consistency: when this is effected the sauce is passed through a tammy cloth.

Various Kinds of Sauces: Having explained the difference between white and brown sauces, and having given minute details of the various thickenings (liaisons), as well as other important points concerning sauces and their preparation, I will now give a list of the various sauces which are most frequently used in cookery.

There are two groups of sauces:

I. Hot Sauces: These are divided into three sections:

(1) Plain.　　(2) Savory.　　(3) Sweet.

II. Cold Sauces: These are divided into three sections:

(1) Chaud-froid.　(2) Salad.　(3) Sweet.

I. Hot Sauces.

(1) PLAIN SAUCES.—These include:

Melted Butter	White Sauce	Mustard
Anchovy	Parsley	Caper Sauce
Brown	Onion (white	Fennel
Egg	or brown)	Bread, etc.

(2) SAVORY SAUCES.—(a) WHITE SAUCES:

Béchamel	Dutch or	Horse-radish
Cream	Hollandaise	Maitre d'Hôtel
Oyster	Lobster	Pluche
Mussel	Normande	Béarnaise
Poulette	Ravigote	Chicken
Fines Herbes	Shrimp	Suprême
Soubise	Provençale	Cucumber
Cardinal	Celery	Mousseline, etc
Mornay	Echalotte	
Veloutée	Allemande	

(b) BROWN SAUCES:

Espagnole	Italienne	Madère
Bordelaise	Bretonne	Génoise
Curry	Financière	Lyonnaise
Chasseur	Robert	Tomato
Matelotte	Milanaise	Bigarade
Mushroom	Olive	Périgord
Orange	Réforme	Game
Truffle	Poivrade	Estragon, etc.
Pompadour	Salmis	
Turtle	Piquante	

(3) SWEET SAUCES:

Apple	Peach	Gooseberry
Apricot	Vanilla	Sabayon
Mousseline	Orange	Raspberry
Cherry	German	Strawberry
Chocolate	Custard	Etc.

II. Cold Sauces.

(1) CHAUD-FROIDS:

White	Green	Tomate
Fawn	Brown	Verte
Blonde	Ravigote	Red
Horse-radish	Mint	Cream
Fines Herbes	Pink	Suédoise, etc.

(2) SALAD SAUCES:

Mayonnaise	Tartare	Rémoulade
Cardinal	Ravigote	Mousseline
Moutarde	Fines Herbes	Vinaigrette, et

(3) SWEET SAUCES:

Cream	Vanilla	Raspberry
Rum	Apricot	Strawberry
Banana	Pineapple	Chocolate, etc
Custard	Liqueur	
Caramel	Sabayon	

SEASONING AND FLAVORING

The business of an intelligent cook is twofold: he or she must know how to please the eye, but above all the palate must be flattered as well, for "where pleasures to the eye and palate meet, such work is done and the dishes are complete." This is particularly essential in the case of sauces and their making.

The best chefs de cuisine regard seasoning and flavoring ingredients as absolute necessities to carry out their object, because the success of their cooking depends largely upon their aid. But condiments for seasoning and flavoring must be used with skill, and above all sparingly.

All palates do not crave for highly spiced foods, or for condiments, yet the majority of people demand that the food should be moderately seasoned with some kind of condiments, for the flavor of insipid food can be very much improved by the use of some suitable condiment.

To flavor or season rightly is an accomplishment of no mean order. Consider how much food is spoilt through being over-seasoned, and how much of it is made insipid through lack of proper and sufficient seasoning. Almost everything we cook has a flavor of its own, the natural flavor, and to retain this becomes often a difficulty, because the great secret lies in bringing out the natural flavor, rather than imparting a new one.

All those who have been initiated into the rudiments of cookery, as well as connoisseurs, must know that the success of any dish, whether plain or elaborate, depends to a very large extent upon its seasoning, and everyone who desires to master this art must carefully study and observe all the rules pertaining to this important branch of cookery. Intelligence, carefulness, thorough, sound judgment, a steady hand, and a keen perception of palate are qualifications which every cook must possess in order to prepare food so as to make it appetizing, pleasant to the taste, and in every way perfectly palatable. Well cooked and well seasoned food is admittedly more digestible than the unpalatable.

An erroneous idea prevails that "plain cookery" requires no other flavoring or seasoning beyond salt, pepper, and, say, Worcester sauce or ketchup. It can easily be proved that there are a variety of inexpensive seasonings besides these which may with advantage be used for imparting a better flavor, whereby the monotony of plain dishes becomes considerably alleviated.

It is most difficult to give any precise directions for seasoning; experience alone will teach a cook. Tastes differ considerably. What may be agreeable to one may be objectionable or insipid to another. It is the cook's business to study the taste of those he or she serves, and the seasoning of the food must therefore be used according to the requirements of those to whom the dishes are served.

It is in all cases well to remember that seasonings, whatever they may consist of, should be used in small quantities only, as one can always add more if found necessary, but it is impossible to remove any if too much has been added in the first instance.

The late Monsieur Ude, one of the most talented chefs of the past, in his culinary work says that "the best cookery in the world is worthless without seasoning."

We know that cookery acts upon food by diminishing the firmness of some articles, and by increasing it in others. We further know that the flavor is altered as well as the aroma and appearance, whilst seasoning and flavoring heighten the savoriness of food, the action of which is increased by the addition of aromatic, pungent, and stimulant ingredients. The so-called highly seasoned dishes must be regulated on a sliding scale as regards the seasoning employed, so as to adapt them to the various palates, which, as before stated, differ considerably. It is quite impossible to specify in any recipe the exact quantity of seasoning materials for each dish. Not only palates but also stomachs differ as to the amount of salt and spices which suits them. For this reason, if for no other, it is always best to use all seasonings moderately. The object of seasoning, providing always it be added in moderate and reasonable quantities, is to increase the digestibility of food, to flavor food which would otherwise be insipid, and to render it at the same time more palatable and digestible. By seasoning certain food materials, we copy to a certain extent nature, who renders fruit wholesome and agreeable to the taste by associating insipidness with acids, by combining certain forms of starch with sugar, as well as by the characteristic instinctive longing with which nature animates both man and animal for salt and for the flavor and piquancy of aromatic herbs and spices.

While a fine and discriminating taste is natural to a few only, it may be cultivated in some degree by all. It is the fortune of the cook who possesses it; if not, he or she may, through plenty of experience, acquire it in some measure.

The most important articles used for seasoning and flavoring are salt, sugar, pepper, spices, aromatic herbs, vinegar, vegetables, mustard, butter and other fats, oils, etc. The principal functions which these adjuncts have to perform is, as explained in the foregoing pages, to render food more palatable, more appetizing, and more digestible.

Salt is the chief and most important seasoning used; it is not merely a seasoning, but a necessary of life, for it removes the insipid flavor from all eatables, such as meat, vegetables, etc.; it acts as an appetizer, and promotes digestion. The average quantity of salt required by each person being, according to medical authority, from ¼ to ½ an ounce per day, it becomes a necessary adjunct for the preservation of health. When added to food it excites the supply of two important agents in the processes of digestion and nutrition, viz., the gastric juice and the constituents of the bile. Salt, like all seasonings, must be used with judgment.

When added to boiling water, it raises the boiling-point and liberates the oxygen. Salt acts further as a great preserving agent for meat, vegetables, and other substances.

Spices, such as white and black pepper, cayenne, cloves, nutmeg, paprika (Hungarian pepper), coriander, cinnamon, mace, etc., cannot be considered to have any nutritive properties. They are used for the purpose of imparting certain flavors to improve the taste of various food substances. In adding the seasoning and flavoring to dishes, it is of the greatest importance for a cook to remember that the exquisite sensibility of a cook's palate can best be judged and admired by his or her cooking.

Allspice: This well-known and useful spice is the berry of the "Eugenia Pimenta," a small tree growing in the West Indies. The fruit is gathered when green and unripe, and put to dry in the sun, when it turns black. Large quantities of it are employed in the manufacture of the sauces sold in shops. The berries combine the flavor of cloves, cinnamon, and nutmeg, hence the name allspice. It is also called Pimento or Jamaica pepper.

Cloves: Cloves belong to the order of myrtles. They are the unopened flower-buds of a plant called the "Caryophyllus aromaticus," a native of the Moluccas. Owing to their resemblance to a nail they derive their name from the French word "clou." They form a well-known spice, and are much used in cookery, both in sweet and savory dishes. To a stew or ragoût, etc., an onion stuck with cloves is almost indispensable.

Nutmeg: Used extensively for various seasonings, both sweet and savory. It is the seed of the nutmeg-tree [Myristica moschata], a native of the Molucca Islands, but is now cultivated in Java, Cayenne, Sumatra, and some of the West Indian Islands. The fruit is surrounded by a husk [arillus], which is known as mace. The nutmeg is pear-like in appearance, and is usually grated for culinary purposes. Nutmegs should never be used in large proportions for seasoning because they are supposed to contain narcotic properties.

Mace is the outer shell or husk of the nutmeg, and it resembles it in flavor. When good it should be orange-yellow in color. Used whole or powdered for both seasoning and flavoring.

Curry is a condiment and a spice, but is, strictly speaking, a mixture of many others. Perhaps only an Indian can make it to perfection, many of its ingredients being native to the country, whose poorest peasantry look upon curry as a daily necessity.

Mustard: There are two varieties of mustard seeds, "Sinapis nigra," the black, and "Sinapis alba," the white. These are ground and mixed. The pungency of mustard is more fully developed when moistened with water. It is supposed to give energy to the digestive organs, and to promote appetite if taken in small quantities. It is used as a table condiment, and for sauces, dressings, etc.

Cinnamon: This substance comes from the bark of a species of laurel, "Laurus Cinnamomum," and is about the oldest known spice in the world. The tree is chiefly cultivated in Ceylon, but cinnamon also comes from Madras, Java, and Bombay. The three-year-old branches are stripped of the outer bark, the inner is loosened and dried, which makes it shrivel up, and assume the quill form in which it is imported. The best cinnamon should not be too dark in color, and should be hardly thicker than paper. It has a fragrant odor, and its taste is pleasant and highly aromatic. Besides being used extensively for culinary purposes, cinnamon is much employed medicinally as a powerful stimulant.

Turmeric: Turmeric [Curcuma longa] belongs to the ginger family, and is extensively cultivated in the East Indies as a condiment. The tubers are dried and then ground to a fine powder. It enters largely into the composition of curry powder, and gives it the peculiar odor and the bright yellow color which that compound possesses.

Coriander: This is the fruit or so-called seeds of a plant of Eastern origin [Coriandrum sativum]. Coriander seeds are used by the confectioner and distiller, and in the manufacture of curry powder. The leaves have also been used in soups and salads. They are also used for flavoring jellies, etc.

Aromatic Spice is a mixture of various flavors, consisting of pepper, salt, cinnamon, mace, powdered bayleaf, thyme, marjoram, nutmeg, and cayenne. These are used principally for braised meats, sautés, ragoûts, galantines, vol-au-vents, game pies, and numerous other preparations.

Pepper: Pepper is produced from the seed or berries of the plant or shrub known by the name of "Piper nigrum," which grows in Malabar and various parts of India. The berry has a dark brown or black cuticle. "Black pepper" consists of the dried berries ground whole, whilst "white pepper" is produced from the same berries, after their dark husks have been removed, and ground finely. White pepper is milder than black pepper.

Pepper was known to the ancient Greeks, and so highly was it thought of, that when Alaric besieged Rome in 408 A. D., he included in the ransom 3,000 pounds of pepper.

As a condiment, pepper is valuable in heightening the flavor and giving piquancy to savory dishes, and it behooves a cook to know just what pepper should be used for each dish, for by the use or abuse of this sort of seasoning it is quite possible to make or mar the happiness of a dinner.

Long Pepper [Piper longum] is a spice similar in taste and smell to the ordinary pepper in common use. It is not so pungent; it is mostly used in making curry powder and in pickles. The plant on which it grows is a native of East India.

Mignonette Pepper: This is ordinary white pepper with the husks removed, and crushed finely but not ground.

Cayenne Pepper consists of a species of the dried fruit of capsicums, which is red in color and grows principally in Cayenne. The pods are also imported under the name of "chillies." It has a powerful pungent flavor, and is very useful for flavoring purposes. It also enters into the composition of curry powder.

The plant has been acclimatized in Europe, and its pods are used for pickling, and sometimes for flavoring sauces and stews.

Krona Pepper is a bright red pepper made from the Hungarian paprika, capsicum pod, etc. It is much milder than cayenne, and not in the least pungent. It forms one of the most palatable seasonings for the cuisine and table.

A Pinch of Salt or Pepper: This expression is much used in cookery; it is therefore necessary, in order to convey a notion of the accurate quantities of a pinch, to state that a pinch of salt or pepper should be ⅛ of an ounce, and a small pinch (mostly applied to cayenne) ₁′₆ of an ounce in weight. It would, however, be difficult and impracticable to make use of the scales every time a pinch of salt or pepper is required. The best plan is to ascertain the capacity of one's fingers by weighing the quantity they hold, and then getting accustomed to the exact quantity required for seasoning.

In the matter of spices, as well as of herbs and soup vegetables, it is best to avoid continually referring to the scales, to accustom oneself as much as possible to be able to tell by sight the weight of the needful quantity of ingredients required.

Aromatic Herbs and Plants: The following are the names of herbs and plants mostly used in the kitchen: Parsley, bay-leaves, thyme, marjoram, sage, tarragon, chervil, chives, onions, shallots, garlic, etc. A number of these are used in a dry state, but either dry or fresh they are used in a large variety of preparations.

The Bouquet Garni is the mainstay of the French cuisine, and well it may be; it is more delicate and subtle than spices or dried condiments are apt to be. Usually the bouquet garni is composed of sprigs of chervil, chives, thyme, bay-leaves, tarragon, and parsley.

Parsley possesses a wonderful property of absorbing or masking the taste of stronger flavor-

ing ingredients, so much so that an overdose of
this herb is likely to overpower the more delicate aromas of seasonings. There is no herb
which plays such an important part in cookery
as parsley. Not only does it give the finishing
touch to many sauces and stews, but it is the
favorite for garnishing dishes. The curled leaf
parsley is the best and most often used both for
flavor and appearance. Parsley is said to be a
native of Sardinia, but is largely cultivated in
every country in Europe. Powdered parsley is
excellent for a number of dishes for imparting
a most delicate flavor. The process is simple.
Steep some fresh parsley in boiling water for a
few seconds; then drain and put it in a hot
oven for a few minutes to dry. Put through a
sieve and use as required.

Tarragon and Chervil: Tarragon belongs to
the same family as wormwood, and is called by
botanists "Artemisia Dracunculus." It is supposed to be a native of Siberia. The leaves of
chervil possess a peculiar flavor, which is much
appreciated by many. Of all the pot-herbs.
these two are the most odoriferous, and are much
used in French cookery in entrées and sauces,
and sometimes soups. In salads, salad sauces,
chaud-froid, etc., they also form an important
part. Tarragon-leaves are also used for flavoring
vinegar, which is very largely used in all kitchens and dining-rooms.

Thyme: Thyme belongs to the same family as
mint, the "Labiatæ." The leaves of this plant
[Thymus vulgaris] are used fresh or dry for
stuffing, soups, etc. It possesses a highly aromatic flavor, and should be used sparingly. The
lemon thyme [Thymus citriodorus] is a smaller
kind, and has a strong perfume like the rind of
lemons, which is very agreeable.

Burnet: The use of this perennial plant has
gone somewhat out of fashion. In former times
it made one of the principal ingredients in
claret cup, its leaves, when slightly bruised,
smelling like cucumber. Its modern use is con-
fined to salads, and combined with tarragon,
chives. and chervil. burnet forms the French

"ravigote." Although called "pimprenelle" in French, it must not be confused with the Eng-lish pimpernel, which is poisonous.

Capsicums: Of these there are several kinds which are cultivated in the East and West Indies and in America. They yield a fruit which is pungent and stimulating, and in Mexico the pods are called chillies; these are used to make a hot pickle and chilli vinegar. It is the powder of the seeds and pods dried that constitutes cayenne pepper. Capsicums owe their power to an active principle called capsicin, and are con-sidered to be very wholesome.

Savory: Of this flavoring herb there are two varieties, the summer savory [Satureja hor-tensis] and the winter savory [Satureja mont-ana]. It was introduced into England in the seventeenth century. Both varieties are exten-sively used for flavoring and seasoning purposes.

Marjoram: There are four kinds of marjoram, but the sweet or knotted marjoram [Origanum Majorana], a native of Portugal, and introduced into this country in the sixteenth century, is the kind generally used in our kitchens. It imparts a delicious flavor to soups, sauces, stews, etc. In July the leaves are dried and kept for winter use.

Mint: Mint belongs to a family of plants called "Labiatae". The spearmint [Mentha viridis] cultivated in our gardens has the most agreeable flavor of the various kinds of mint, and is the one most generally used in cookery. It possesses the property of correcting flatu-lency, hence the custom of using it in pea-soup and with new potatoes, etc.

Bay-leaves: The leaves of the common laurel [Prunus Laurocerasus] are employed for culinary purposes to give a kernel-like flavor to stocks, mirepoix, sauces, custards, puddings, blanc-manges, and the milk and water with which cakes are mixed. They are generally dried for use.

Basil: This is a favorite herb with the French cooks; it has a scent very like that of cloves. Basil for winter use can be obtained in bottles, and it is the best herb for clear mock-turtle and other clear soups made of shell-fish. It is also used for flavoring vinegar. The middle of August is the best time for making basil vinegar.

Onions: The name onion is given to all plants of the onion tribe, in which we include leek, garlic and shallot (échalote). The onion is, undoubtedly, next to salt, the most valuable of all flavoring substances used in cookery.

When onions, shallots or garlic are used, they should always be well blended with other flavors, so that the peculiar and often objectionable taste of these cannot be detected.

The smell of the onion, however, is objectionable to many, whilst others will have it that the flavor of onion disagrees with them. The question, therefore arises, how can this be overcome? The answer is very simple. By thorough cooking and manipulation the presence of onion in a stew, soup or sauce may be disguised, retaining at the same time the essential essence of this valuable flavoring root. By cunningly concealing the flavor with others in a sauce, stew or soup, it will yield enjoyment even to those who would carefully avoid it if they knew it was there. Whenever onion is used as a condiment or seasoning, and the article is properly treated as a flavoring substance should be, much of the objection of an unpleasant smell is removed. Too much attention cannot be bestowed upon its preparation.

Garlic: This is one of the alliaceous plants. It consists of a group of several bulbs called "cloves," all enclosed in one membranous skin. When used judiciously and sparingly, garlic is a most excellent condiment; but with the English taste it seldom finds favor, although many without knowing it partake of dishes where it is cunningly concealed. Rubbing the dish once with a clove of garlic cut in half imparts quite sufficient flavor; but in Italy and other countries it is used on a larger scale—in fact, it enters into the composition of nearly every dish. Garlic is considered to be very wholesome, and to act as a slight stimulant and tonic.

Shallot: This bulbous root resembles garlic, and belongs to the same genus. It is a native of Palestine, and was introduced into England by the Crusaders. The place in Palestine where it was first found was Ascalon: hence its botanical name, ''Allium ascalonicum.'' The shallot is extremely useful in cookery, especially for flavoring sauces, vinegar, etc. It is more pungent than garlic, but of more delicate flavor, and consequently more popular than the former.

Carrots and Turnips: Next to the onion, the carrot and turnip are considered the most important flavoring vegetables for soups and sauces. Carrots were known in the time of Elizabeth, and in the reign of James I. they were looked upon as most uncommon and as a luxury, so much so that ladies wore them as a decoration in place of feathers upon their hats and sleeves. Besides their use for flavoring, carrots and turnips are largely used for garnishing certain dishes, such as ragoûts, boiled meats, etc. They are also served as vegetables by themselves, also as purées for soups, etc. It will thus be seen that the humble onion, carrot and turnip are most important in the preparation of many dishes; and in addition to these there is the bouquet garni, the parsley root, so-called pot-herbs, and numerous others, each of which has its special value, the characteristic of which every cook should be fully acquainted with. But, let me repeat, strongly flavored herbs, as well as so-called pot or soup vegetables, should always be used with moderation and judgment.

Vinegar: Vinegar is derived from a variety of sources. The best vinegar is the French vinaigre d'Orléans. It is made from white wine; but common vinegar is mostly prepared from malt in this country. The uses to which vinegar is applied in cookery are very numerous; it forms the foundation of many sauces, and if taken with food in small quantity it is said to assist digestion. If taken, however, in excess, it is highly injurious. Owing to its antiseptic and agreeable flavor, it is largely used for preserving vegetable substances known under the name of "pickles." It also has the faculty of softening the fibres of meat and making them tender.

Sugar is largely used for fruits of all kinds, and farinaceous foods; besides seasoning tasteless things, sugar also affords considerable nutriment. The value of sugar as a condiment is not always sufficiently realized. It renders watery and insipid vegetables more digestible, and in unsuspected quantities it softens and heightens the flavor of sauces and ragoûts. If mingled with otherwise insipid food articles, it stimulates the stomach to a slight degree, and hastens the action of the digestive organs. Sugar is also found useful in rendering watery vegetables, such as peas, cucumbers, pumpkins, spinach, cooked endive, etc., more digestible, and in the same manner assists digestion of starchy matters which are used for soups, sauces, gruel, etc.

Lemons: Lemons play an important part in sauce and other cookery. The rind, juice, and essential oil all contain valuable properties. The rind or peel is used for flavoring a variety of dishes. As a rule the rind is grated, but the best way to obtain the largest amount of the essence from the lemon is to pare the rind with a very sharp knife as thinly as possible, without encroaching on the white part of the rind, thus cutting right through the many cells containing the essence. Some cooks obtain the zest by rubbing the lemon with lumps of sugar. It is from the rind that the essential oil of lemon is obtained, which is a more reliable substitute than fresh lemon peel. The rind preserved with sugar forms the well-known candied peel.

Vanilla: Vanilla was first discovered by the Spaniards. It is the fruit of a parasitical plant —an orchid—and the best is found in Mexico. It has a delicious fragrance, and is now largely used for flavoring puddings, cakes, custards, liqueurs, chocolate, etc. For flavoring purposes it is better to use the vanilla pods or vanilla sugar than the essence of vanilla, the odor of which quickly escapes.

Ginger: Ginger is the tuber of a perennial

plant called "Zingiber officinale," growing chiefly in the West Indies. It is the most generally used of all spices, and is very agreeable and wholesome. There are two kinds of ginger —the white and the black. The former is considered the best, and is prepared by washing and scalding the tubers, and then scraping them and drying them in the sun; in black ginger the scraping process is omitted, it being merely scalded before being dried. Ginger is much used in culinary operations, especially by confectioners, and it also finds its way into sauces, beer, spiced wines and other beverages.

HINTS ON STOCK MAKING.

Use only fresh ingredients such as meat, vegetables, etc., in proper proportion.

Boil up the stock daily and keep it in earthenware pans, not in metal stewpans or pots.

Remove the fat as soon as it congeals on the surface of a stock.

The removal of fat is most essential to all finished stocks and finished sauces alike. Sauces, no matter what kind, should never be greasy. It is strongly advisable that stock for sauces should be prepared the day before it is required.

If this advice be followed a great deal of labor may be saved, and better results will be obtained. Stock loses nothing if kept for two days, provided it be put away in clean vessels (earthenware pans).

Stock for Sauces: A great many of the recipes for sauces direct the use of stock because by its use they are made much richer and more nourishing than when water is used.

Stock is the liquor in which fresh meat, bones, and vegetables have been boiled long enough to extract the goodness therefrom.

To make a useful stock, cut up the meat or meat trimmings and chop the bones; put them in a stock-pot or large stewpan and fill up with cold water, allowing a quart to each pound of meat and bones: add a little salt, and allow it to come to the boil slowly. Then remove the scum, and add stock vegetables, such as carrot, turnip, onion, celery leaves, and parsley root if handy, all of which must have been previously prepared, cleaned and washed. Cook, i. e., simmer, gently for about three or four hours, then strain for use, but be sure that every particle of fat is removed. Almost any kind of meat (cooked or raw), bones, and gravy from roast meat may be used for stock making so long as they are fresh and sweet.

Preparations made from Stocks are summarized as follows: First stock (bouillon or broth). Second or general stock (remouillage); this is a refill of the first stock. Essences. Half-glaze (demi-glaçe) a reduction of first or second stock; and lastly, glaze.

Fish Stock: This can be made of almost any kind of fish, but oily fish should be avoided. Fish broth, all know, is particularly nourishing, light and digestible. Thick-skinned fish always make the best broth.

The following is an excellent stock:

Take 2 lbs. fish and fish bones, set it in a pot with two quarts of water, an onion stuck with two cloves, a few peppercorns, mace, and a bouquet. Skim as it comes to a boil, and allow it to reduce to about half its quantity by very slow simmering. A little white wine or vinegar is often put with this stock. Wine gives a specially nice flavor to fish broth. Salt must be added at the last moment.

AUXILIARY RECIPES FOR SAUCES.

Bouquet garni: This item is used in several of the sauce recipes; it is often called a bunch of herbs, or a fagot of sweet herbs, and is much used in all kinds of meat cookery where savory flavor is desired. Many people praise the flavor of French soups and sauces, the delicious aromatic flavor of which is generally due to the use of a bouquet of herbs or a bouquet garni, which enters largely into the composition of many of the French preparations, soups, ragoûts and sauces. To make a bouquet garni, lay upon the left hand a few branches of fresh parsley well washed, and place upon this a sprig of thyme, a sprig of marjoram, a bay-leaf, a sprig of basil, a celery leaf and a small piece of cinnamon stick, also a clove of garlic if liked, together with a small blade of mace and a pepper pod (long pepper). Fold the parsley round the other herbs, etc., and tie with a string into a neat little bunch (bouquet) and use as directed. Excessive use of strong-smelling herbs or spices must in all cases be avoided.

Meat Glaze (Glace de Viande): Put 8 quarts of good stock, white or brown, into a stewpan, boil up, skim well, and reduce on a moderate fire from 3½ to 4 hours. It will make barely half a pint when done. Put into a jar whilst hot, cover and keep in a dry place, and use as required. If well made it will keep for a long time.

Duxelle Purée (Required: 2 oz. butter, 2 oz. finely chopped cooked ham, 6 mushrooms, 3 shallots, 1 clove garlic, 1 truffle, 1 glass of white wine stock, bay-leaf, pepper, salt, nutmeg, allemande sauce).

Chop the mushrooms, shallots, a few sprigs of parsley, garlic, and the truffle. Melt the butter in a stewpan, add the ham and the above-named ingredients, stir over the fire for a few minutes, moisten with a glass of white wine and a little stock, season with pepper, salt, nutmeg and a little powdered bay-leaf; when well reduced stir in four tablespoonfuls of allemande sauce, boil again, and serve as required.

Fumet of Game (Fumet de Gibier): Carcass of game, 1 small carrot, ½ onion, 1 bay-leaf, 1 sprig of thyme, 2 oz. raw ham, 1 oz. lard or butter, 1 glass sherry, 1 quart stock.

Chop up the carcass, wash, peel and slice the carrot, peel and slice the onion. Put the butter or lard in a stewpan, when hot add the carcass and ham cut into small pieces, fry a few minutes, then add the vegetables and herbs. Fry again, moisten with the wine, cover, and steam a few minutes, add the stock and cook for twenty minutes. Skim, strain, and use as directed.

Chicken Essence (Essence de Volaille): Reduce 1 quart of chicken stock or consommé over a slow fire to about half a pint. Skim, strain into a white pot, and use as required.

Meat Juice: (This is sometimes used to enrich certain sauces.) To extract the juice from meat, a special press is required. The meat intended for this purpose must be very underdone.

Venison and ducks, beef fillets and carcasses, are frequently treated in this way.

Raw, lean beef when required for raw beef juice should be well batted, freed from skin and fat, and cut into strips before being put into the press.

Chopped Parsley (Persil haché): Wash some parsley, trim off some of the stalks if coarse, chop as finely as possible, place it in the corner of a clean cloth, fold the end of the cloth, and hold tightly under the water-tap or rinse in a basin of cold water, squeeze out all the water, and put the parsley on a plate till wanted.

To Chop an Onion: Peel the onion, cut it in two lengthways, leaving the stalk ends. Commence to slice each half without detaching the slices from the stalk. Keep firmly together, and cut through several times crossways; then cut down horizontally into fine squares, until you come to the stalk. This is the quickest way to mince an onion, but it requires practice. The other way is to peel and chop in the ordinary manner. When fine enough, wash in cold water, drain on a cloth, and use as required.

To Chop Mushrooms: If freshly gathered mushrooms are used, peel off the skins, trim the stalks, and wash in cold water; then chop as required and use immediately.

Preserved mushrooms are well drained, and then chopped as required.

Liaisons in general (for thickening of sauces): There are a number of processes of thickening soups and sauces, and these are called "liaisons," in a culinary sense.

Liaison may be composed of flour (fécule, arrowroot, cornflour, crème-de-riz, etc.), diluted in either milk, cream, stock or water, according to the nature of the soup or sauce for which it is required. A liaison should always be strained before it is mixed with the liquid which requires thickening, and the preparation be well stirred whilst the latter is added.

The liaison of egg is frequently used for white purées, blanquettes, fricassées and white sauces.

Only the yolks of eggs should be used, mixed with a small quantity of cream, and well beaten.

Such liaison should only be added to the preparation for which it is required when it is thoroughly cooked; part of the soup or sauce is poured on to the liaison, stirred and then all mixed well together.

When once the liaison of egg is added, the preparation must on no account be allowed to boil, but only just get thoroughly heated, so as to form the liaison, thus preventing the eggs from curdling.

How to Tammy Sauces: Some of the more delicate compound sauces are frequently strained through a tammy cloth, so as to render them as smooth or creamlike as possible. To effect this process two persons are needed who take hold of the tammy cloth on both ends; the liquid or purée to be passed is then poured in the cloth, each holds a wooden spoon with the right hand and the end of the cloth with the left hand, and both spoons are pressed backward and forward, in regular motion, till the bulk of the liquid has passed through.

Liquid Caramel: (for coloring sauces.) Put a pound of loaf, castor or moist sugar into a copper stewpan or sugar-boiler. Add about half a gill of water, and let it dissolve slowly, then stir over a slow fire and cook until a dark brown color; when a whitish smoke appears it is a sign that the sugar is done. Remove it from the fire, pour on about a pint of boiling water, allow this to boil up whilst stirring, and cook till it has the appearance of a syrup; when cool put it in a corked bottle and use as required.

Caramel should be used with discretion. Good cooks rarely use it, for it is apt to impart a bitter taste if used too freely. It is principally used for coloring, gravies and sauces.

Aspic or Savory Jelly: (used for certain Cold sauces for chaud froids, etc): Required: 1 quart clear stock or water, 2½ oz. gelatine, the juice of 1 lemon and its rind, ½ gill sherry, ½ gill tarragon vinegar, ½ gill French wine or Orléans vinegar, 1 small bunch of herbs, (bouquet garni), 1 small onion sliced, 1 bay-leaf, 10 peppercorns, 10 allspice, 1 blade of mace, a few celery leaves, ½ small carrot, sliced, ½ teaspoonful salt, the whites and shells of 2 eggs.

See that all the ingredients are ready and the vegetables clean. Whisk up lightly the whites of eggs with the shells, and put them, together with the remainder of the above-named ingredients, into a well-tinned stewpan, stir with a whisk over the fire, and bring it thus slowly to boil. Remove the whisk and draw the stewpan away from the fire, and allow it to simmer gently on the side of the stove for about twenty minutes. Strain through a clean cloth previously steeped in boiling water and tied over a soup stand or the legs of a stool upside down; or pass it through a warm jelly-bag; if not clear at first, pass it through a second or third time. The aspic is then ready for use. This aspic is suitable for borders or decorative purposes; if required for other purposes, 2 ounces of gelatine will be found sufficient.

SAVORY OR COMPOUND SAUCES

Used for Fish, Meat, Poultry, Game and Certain Vegetables.

Admiral Sauce (Sauce à l'Amiral): To one pint of rich white sauce (velouté or allemande) add 1 dessertspoonful of finely chopped capers, 1 teaspoonful of chopped parsley, one of chopped lemon rind, the juice of half a lemon, and a teaspoonful of anchovy essense. Reheat and serve hot.

Aigre-Douce Sauce: ¾ pint poivrade sauce, 1 tablespoonful red-currant jelly, 2 tablespoonfuls cream.

To the poivrade sauce add the red-currant jelly,

boil up and skim, then stir in the cream, reheat without boiling again, season to taste and use as required. This sauce is especially suitable for roast game, etc.

Albany Sauce: Peel thinly one small cucumber, cut it into small pieces, cook till tender in salted water, then drain, and rub through a fine sieve. When cold stir in a purée made with one teaspoonful of anchovy essence, a tablespoonful of tarragon vinegar, a dessertspoonful of chutney, a dessertspoonful of finely chopped gherkins, half a pint of mayonnaise, half a gill of aspic jelly, half a gill of cream, paprika pepper, a little salt, and a pinch of castor sugar. Mix all well together and add a few drops of spinach greening to give it a green tint.

Albert Sauce: Prepare a Sauce Bérnaise, but substitute the tarragon with a few finely-chopped leaves of green mint, and add a little finely-grated horse-radish.

Albufera Sauce: Prepare a rich supreme sauce, and flavor it with liquefied meat extract or glaze.

Allemande Sauce: 1½ oz. butter, 1 oz. flour, 2 yolks of eggs, 1 tablespoonful of cream, 1 teaspoonful lemon juice, chicken stock, nutmeg, salt, pepper.

Melt the butter in a stewpan, add the flour, stir a few minutes without allowing it to brown, dilute with rather more than a pint of chicken stock, and stir until it boils. Season with pepper and salt and grated nutmeg. Let it simmer for half an hour, skim, and finish with liaison made of the yolks of eggs, the cream, and ½ oz. of fresh butter. Stir over the fire until the eggs begin to set, but do not let it boil; add the lemon juice, and pass through fine strainer or tammy cloth.

American Sauce (Sauce Americaine): Heat up some tomato sauce and blend it with lobster butter sufficient to flavor and color, which must be whisked in.

Anchovy Sauce (Sauce Anchois): 1 oz. butter, ¾ oz. flour, ½ pint milk, ¼ pint fish stock, 1 dessertspoonful anchovy essence.

Melt the butter in a stewpan, stir in the flour, mix well and cook a little. Add by degrees the milk and the fish stock. Stir till it boils, and let cook for 10 minutes. Incorporate a small dessertspoonful of anchovy essence, boil up again and strain.

Another Way: Heat up half a pint of béchamel or hollandaise sauce, and stir in one teaspoonful of anchovy essence.

Anchovy Cream (Crème d'Anchois): Whip up a gill of cream and add to it a tablespoonful of anchovy essence, a teaspoonful of made mustard, a pinch of paprika pepper, and if liked a few drops of liquid carmine. When sufficiently whipped put the cream into a sauceboat, and serve with grilled or boiled fish such as salmon, turbot or soles.

Anchovy Egg Sauce (Sauce anchois aux oeufs): Melt 1 oz. of butter in a saucepan, stir in 1 oz. of flour and cook without browning; then add 1 teaspoonful of anchovy essence, half a pint of boiling milk, and a similar quantity of white stock; stir until the sauce is smooth. Next add a fine-chopped hard-boiled egg, a pinch of cayenne, and about 2 tablespoonfuls of cream.

Aspic Mayonnaise: ½ pint aspic jelly, 1 gill stiff mayonnaise.

Dissolve the aspic and let it get partially cool, then stir it gently into the mayonnaise and use before it begins to set, according to direction.

Aspic à la Tomate (Tomato Aspic): 1 pint aspic jelly, 4 small ripe tomatoes or ½ pint tomato pulp, ½ oz. French leaf gelatine, 1 dessertspoonful sherry.

Blanch and peel the tomatoes, rub through a fine hair sieve, dissolve the gelatine, and add to the pulp. Put the jelly, tomato pulp, and sherry in a stew pan, boil up, skim well, and simmer for a few minutes; pass all through a fine hair sieve, and use as directed.

Aurora Sauce: 1 pint of béchamel sauce, 2 oz. butter, 1 oz. lobster butter, ½ gill cream, 1 dessertspoonful tarragon vinegar, cayenne.

Put the béchamel sauce in a stewpan, add the

butter, a pinch of cayenne, cream, tarragon vinegar, and lobster butter. Stir well over boiling water till hot, but without letting the sauce boil.

Aurora Sauce (No. 2): Mix a gill of béchamel sauce with the juice of half a lemon, a tablespoonful of mushroom liquor, and half a gill of cream. Stir over the fire till it boils, then add two hard-boiled egg-yolks rubbed through a sieve, and finish with an ounce of lobster butter or crayfish butter.

Avignonese Sauce (Sauce Avignonnaise): This consists of béchamel sauce enriched with yolks of eggs and grated parmesan, to which is added chopped parsley; a flavor of shallots or garlic is liked by some, and incorporated accordingly.

Ayola Sauce: This consists of a mayonnaise flavored with finely crushed garlic just sufficient to taste, and lemon juice.

Bâtarde Sauce (Hot): This consists of English melted butter sauce enriched with chicken veloutée and flavored with lemon juice.

Bâtarde Sauce (Cold): Prepare a Béarnaise sauce, flavor it with fish essence or fumet de poisson enriched with tomato purée and anchovy butter.

Bavaroise Sauce: Prepare a Hollandaise or Dutch sauce, and stir in some whipped cream and sufficient crayfish butter to flavor and color.

Béarnaise Sauce: ½ gill tarragon vinegar, 3 shallots finely chopped, 6 peppercorns, crushed, 4 yolks of eggs, 1 tablespoonful of white sauce, 4 oz. butter, 1 sprig thyme, meat glaze, and lemon-juice.

Put the shallots, peppercorns and thyme with the vinegar in a stewpan, cover and boil until well reduced, remove the thyme, add the sauce and a little dissolved meat glaze. Whisk in the yolks of eggs, taking care not to let the sauce boil, remove the stewpan from the fire, and work in by degrees the butter. Only a little butter must be added at a time, otherwise the sauce will get oily. Strain through a pointed strainer or tammy. A little finely chopped fresh tarragon and chervil, and a few drops of lemon-juice may be added after the sauce is strained.

Béarnaise Sauce (Brune): Prepare an ordinary Béarnaise as above, with the addition of meat glaze to give it a brown color.

Béarnaise Sauce (Tomatée): Same as above, adding tomato purée in place of meat glaze.

Béchamel Sauce (White Sauce): Dissolve one ounce of butter in a small stewpan, add one ounce of flour; stir over the fire for a few minutes, just long enough to cook the flour, without allowing it to brown. Stir in a pint of boiling milk; add a small onion stuck with a clove, ten white peppercorns, half a bay-leaf, a sliced carrot, a pinch of salt, and a little grated nutmeg. Stir until it boils, and allow to simmer for fifteen minutes. Pass through a tammy cloth or napkin, return to the stewpan, and finish with a small piece of butter, and half a teaspoonful of lemon juice.

Béchamel Sauce (another way): 1½ oz. flour, 2 oz. butter, 1¼ pint of milk, and white meat stock, 1 small onion or shallot, 1 small bouquet garni, 10 peppercorns, ½ a bay-leaf, 1 small blade of mace, seasoning.

Put the milk on to boil with the onion or shallot (peeled) the bouquet, peppercorns, mace, and bay-leaf. Melt the butter, stir in the flour and cook a little without browning (or use white roux) stir in the milk, etc., (hot), whisk over the fire until it boils, and let simmer from fifteen to twenty minutes. Take out the bouquet, rub through a sieve or tammy, return to the stewpan, season lightly with a pinch of nutmeg, half-pinch of cayenne, and half a teaspoonful of salt. The sauce is then ready for use.

Béchamel Sauce (Maigre): Proceed the same as above directed, omitting the meat stock, and using in its place milk and fish stock or milk and vegetable stock or water.

Beef Marrow Sauce (Sauce Moëlle de Boeuf): Blend some Espagnole sauce with fried shallot, and add blanched beef marrow previously cut in thin slices, also some finely chopped parsley, a little chili vinegar and red pepper to taste. Serve hot.

Beefsteak Sauce: Prepare a light brown sauce of the demi-glace type to which chopped onion and parsley have been added. Enrich this with meat glaze and butter, and flavor with sherry and lemon juice.

Bércy Sauce: Reduce 1½ gills of fish stock to about one-third its quantity, then add 1 chopped shallot, previously tossed in butter, 1 glass white wine, 1 teaspoonful of meat or fish glaze, and reduce again, and add ½ gill of velouté sauce, and the juice of ¼ lemon. Tammy and return to the stewpan, finish with 1 oz. of herb butter and serve.

NOTE: The herb butter is made with finely chopped fennel, tarragon, chervil, and parsley, and fresh butter.

Beurre-Noir Sauce (Black Butter Sauce): 1½ oz. butter, 1 teaspoonful finely chopped parsley, ½ teaspoonful vinegar.

Put the butter in an omelette pan, fry over a quick fire until it acquires a nut-brown color, then add the vinegar and parsley. Pour over the article to be served.

Bigarade Sauce: Proceed the same as for orange sauce, but substitute a Seville orange for a sweet one. Use only half the rind, and boil at least for ten minutes. Omit red-currant jelly, and add a glass of port wine in its place.

Blanquette Sauce: This sauce is made the same as Sauce Allemande, adding three tablespoonfuls of cream instead of one.

Bohemian Sauce (Bohemienne Sauce): Prepare a white sauce with freshly-made breadcrumbs, milk and white stock, stir in fresh butter and finely grated horseradish to flavor, then season with pepper and salt if needed.

Good Woman Sauce (Bonne Femme Sauce): Chop finely one small peeled onion or 3 shallots, blend this in butter in a saucepan; and add half a pint of fish stock. Boil up and reduce with half a pint of Béchamel sauce, then thicken with 2 egg-yolks, season to taste, and flavor with lemon juice; finish the sauce with a little whipped cream.

Bonnefoy Sauce: This consists of a light, well flavored bordelaise sauce (claret flavored brown sauce), into which a little fresh butter, some finely chopped parsley, and purée of beef marrow have been incorporated.

Bordelaise Sauce: ¾ pint espagnole or brown sauce, 1 wineglassful red wine, 2 finely chopped shallots, ½ oz. meat glaze, 1 teaspoonful chopped herbs (parsley, tarragon and chervil) a pinch of sugar, salt and pepper.

Put the wine and shallots in a stewpan, reduce to half, add the sauce, and cook slowly for twenty minutes. Take off the scum, add the chopped herbs and meat glaze. Season with sugar, salt and pepper. Give it one more boil, and keep hot in the bain-marie until required.

Bordelaise Sauce (No. 2): Put into a saucepan a gill of claret, 4 finely chopped and peeled shallots, a few peppercorns, a bayleaf, and a sprig of thyme. Cover, and let it reduce to about half its volume, then add ¾ of a pint of Espagnole or other rich brown sauce. Reduce a little and strain into another saucepan. Stir or whisk in a pat of fresh butter, and a large tablespoonful of beef marrow, previously cut into small dice and poached. The sauce is then ready.

NOTE: In most cases where Bordelaise sauce is used, and especially so with beef, some thin, round slices of beef marrow are blanched and put on the meat before it is served, or else heated up in the sauce.

Bordeaux Sauce: Peel and mince finely two shallots, reduce with 1 gill of claret with ½ a teaspoonful of crushed white peppercorns, a sprig of thyme, and a sprig of marjoram. When about half reduced, add 1 gill of espagnole sauce, and boil for 10 minutes, then strain, re-heat, and whisk in 1 teaspoonful of anchovy or crayfish butter. Season to taste, and use as directed.

Bread Sauce (Sauce au Pain): 4 oz. fresh bread-crumbs, 1 small onion, 1 clove, 4 peppercorns, 1 pint of milk, ½ oz. fresh butter, salt, 2 tablespoonfuls cream.

Peel the onion, stick in it the clove, put the onion and milk in a saucepan, boil up, add the bread-crumbs and the peppercorns, cook for fifteen minutes. Remove the onions and peppercorns, stir in the cream and butter, season with a pinch of salt, and keep hot until required for serving. If liked the onion may be cooked longer, passed through a sieve, and added to the sauce; the cream can be omitted; if found too thick, a little hot water can be added. Bread sauce is usually served with roast fowl, turkey and game birds.

Bread Sauce (No. 2): Peel, slice and mince very finely a small onion; simmer till quite soft in a pint of milk; strain it over about 6 ounces of stale bread, free from crust and broken up small; let it soak for an hour, beat up with a fork, and season with a little nutmeg or ground mace, cayenne and salt. Lastly add an ounce of butter and bring gradually to the boil, stirring all the time.

Bread Sauce (No. 3): Insert two cloves into a small peeled onion, put it into a stewpan with a pint of milk, and let it infuse over a gentle heat for 30 minutes. Take out the onion, add a small cup of breadcrumbs, and season to taste with salt and pepper; boil gently for five minutes, stirring continually, then add half an ounce of butter and a tablespoonful of cream; stir and blend all thoroughly, then serve.

Bread Sauce (No. 4): Put half a pint of milk into a saucepan, to this add the crumb of a dinner roll and a small peeled onion; bring slowly to the boil, stirring occasionally, and cook for 10 minutes. Take out the onion, add an ounce of butter, and season to taste with salt and cayenne and a grate of nutmeg. Beat up well till quite smooth still over the fire, and then serve.

Breton Sauce (Sauce Bretonne): Prepare a pint of brown onion sauce in the usual way, blend it with tomato sauce, and thicken with a little haricot bean purée.

Brown Butter Sauce (Beurre Noir): Take 3 ounces of butter, one tablespoonful of minced parsley, a small dessertspoonful of flour, 3 table-spoonfuls of vinegar, pepper and salt to taste. Mix the butter, flour and parsley together, then put this into a saucepan and stir until it is melted, add salt and pepper to taste and lastly the vinegar, and stir over a rather hot stove for ten minutes.

Brown Fish Sauce (Sauce Brune pour Poisson): ½ lb. fish bones, etc., 1½ oz. butter, 1 dessert-spoonful of flour, one tablespoonful English corn-flour, 1 gill claret (optional), three-quarters pint fish stock or water, 1 sliced onion, 1 small bunch savory herbs (bouquet garni), 4 mush-rooms, salt and pepper to taste.

Fry the fish-bones, etc., in the butter over a quick fire, add the onion and fry also, stir in the flour and cornflour, and let the flour get brown whilst stirring; add the carrot, herbs, and mush-rooms, and moisten with the claret and the stock. Stir till it boils and let simmer for twenty minutes. Pass through a tammy cloth or fine sieve, season to taste, and serve. If liked the mushrooms may be chopped finely and put into the sauce at the last.

Cold Bulgarian Sauce No. 2 (Bulgare Sauce): This can also be made with a cold tomato sauce, blended with a little mayonnaise, with the addi-tion of a little finely shredded or chopped cooked celery.

Burgundy Sauce (Bourguignonne Sauce): This is a brown sauce composed of Espagnole sauce, to which finely minced onions and parsley, re-duced in Burgundy wine, flavored with thyme, bay-leaf, cloves and mace, have been added. Strain or tammy the sauce, season to taste and serve hot.

Butter Sauce (Sauce au beurre): Put 1½ ounces of butter into a stewpan, together with a grate of nutmeg, and 2 saltspoonfuls of mig-nonette pepper. When the butter is hot add 1 oz. of flour, and cook gently whilst stirring, taking care that the flour does not brown. When thoroughly cooked add not quite 1 pint of boil-ing milk, stirring all the time until it forms the consistency of ordinary white sauce; if strong flour is used it will take a little more moisture. Reduce a little, and then add gradually 4 to 6 ounces of fresh butter, stirring quickly during this operation. Should the sauce appear to turn oily, add a spoonful of cold water, flavor with a little lemon juice and salt, and pass through a tammy. This sauce can be used as foundation for a number of sauces, but it should not be made too long before it is required to be used.

Creamed Butter Sauce (Beurre Crêmeuse Sauce): Beat or whisk 3 egg yolks and add 4 ozs. of butter, stir into it sufficient richly flavored boiling stock. Stir over hot water till a cream-like sauce is obtained.

Byron Sauce: Reduce half a pint of demi-glace sauce with a gill of claret, then add 2 finely chopped truffles, and season to taste.

Calville Sauce: Strain the juice of a lemon and an orange into a clean saucepan, to this add 4 tablespoonfuls of demi-glace or other well-flavored thin brown sauce, a few drops of liquid carmine, a pinch of paprika pepper, half an ounce of meat glaze, and two finely chopped peeled shallots; bring to the boil, skim, add a wine-glass of dry port or Burgundy wine, and a teaspoonful of castor sugar. Serve hot with roast birds, such as teal, sarcelle, or wild duck.

Cambridge Sauce (excellent with Cold Meat or Salad): 4 eggs, 4 fillets of anchovies, 1 tablespoonful of capers, 1 dessertspoonful French mustard, 1 teaspoonful English mustard, 2 tablespoonfuls olive oil, 1 tablespoonful tarragon vinegar, tarragon and chervil, cayenne, parsley or olives.

Pound in a mortar the hard-boiled yolks of eggs, anchovies, capers, a sprig of tarragon and chervil; then add French mustard, English mustard, a pinch of cayenne pepper, and moisten with the olive oil and tarragon vinegar. Rub the whole through a fine tammy or hair sieve, stir in a little more oil and vinegar, and work to the desired consistency; keep it on the ice till wanted, and add a little chopped parsley or olives just before serving. No salt is needed, on account of the anchovies used in making this sauce.

Cambridge Sauce (Cold): To a pint of mayonnaise sauce, add a tablespoonful of parsley purée, a dessertspoonful of finely chopped capers, and a teaspoonful of anchovy paste. Mix well, and flavor with a little made mustard.

Canopère Sauce: This consists of a hot fish sauce made with fish, court-bouillon and blond roux, enriched with sufficient crayfish butter to flavor and color.

Caper Sauce (Sauce aux Câpres): ½ pint melted butter sauce, 1 tablespoonful capers, ½ tablespoonful vinegar.

Mix with the melted butter sauce a tablespoonful of capers and the vinegar. Boil up and serve with boiled fish, mutton, etc.

Brown Caper Sauce (Sauce aux Capres brune): A brown sauce, espagnole or demi-glace containing coarsely chopped capers, seasoned with nutmeg and black pepper.

Cardinal Sauce: ½ pint veloutée or béchamel sauce, 1 oz. butter, juice of ½ lemon, ½ oz. lobster coral or one oz. lobster butter, one dessertspoonful meat glaze, ½ gill mushroom liquor, salt, pepper, nutmeg.

Reduce the sauce with the mushroom liquor, season with salt, pepper, and a grate of nutmeg; add the lemon-juice, and whisk in the butter and lobster butter or coral, the latter finely chopped. Strain or tammy. Return to the stewpan and add the meat glaze, stir till smooth, and keep hot in the bain-marie till required.

NOTE: When this sauce is required for maigre dishes use béchamel maigre sauce in place of veloutée. Omit the meat glaze and add in its place ¼ gill of cream.

Celery Sauce: Trim and wash the white part of a large head of celery, peel a good-sized onion, cut both up small and boil in salted water till tender, drain, and chop very finely. Rub the yolks of two hard-boiled eggs through a sieve, and mix with half a teacupful of cream and a little white stock, add the celery and onion, and a teaspoonful of chilli vinegar. Season to taste with salt and pepper and serve hot or cold.

Celery Cream Sauce (Crème de Céléri): 1 small head of celery, 1 pint milk, 1 oz. butter, 1 oz. flour, a little cream, salt, pepper, and nutmeg.

Remove the best part of the celery, wash well, blanch it, drain and steep in cold water; cut the celery into small pieces, put in a stewpan with the milk, diluted with a little cold stock, add some salt, boil up, skim, and cook till tender. Meanwhile prepare a white roux, i. e. dissolve the butter in a stewpan, add the flour, and stir over the fire until the latter is cooked without browning; then add gradually the celery and stock, let boil a little longer, pass through a tammy cloth, return to the stewpan. Season to taste with salt, pepper, and nutmeg. Stir over the fire until it boils, then add a little cream, and keep in the bain-marie until required.

Champagne Sauce: ¾ pint of espagnole sauce, 1 glass of champagne, 2 cloves, 6 peppercorns, 1 bay-leaf.

Put the cloves, peppercorns, bay-leaf, and espagnole sauce into a stewpan on the fire; let it reduce a little, add the champagne, and the essence remaining from the braised ham. Reduce the whole for ten minutes, or longer if found too thin. Strain through a pointed strainer and serve with braised ham.

White Mushroom Sauce (Sauce Champignons, Blanche): 1½ gill béchamel sauce, 1½ gill white stock, 10 mushrooms, 1 dessertspoonful lemon-juice, white wine, 1 tablespoonful cream.

Boil together the béchamel sauce and the veal stock (or other white stock), and reduce to about half its original quantity. Skim well and add the preserved mushrooms cut into slices, 1 tablespoonful of mushroom liquor, lemon-juice, and about half a gill of Chablis or other white wine. Let the whole boil, season to taste, then add one tablespoonful of cream, and serve.

Brown Mushroom Sauce (Sauce Champignons, brune): ½ pint demi-glace sauce, 1 glass sherry, and 10 champignons (preserved mushrooms).

Chop finely the preserved mushrooms (champignons), put them in a small stewpan with a little of the liquor and the sherry, cover and allow to reduce well. Now add the demi-glace or thin espagnole sauce; boil up, skim, season to taste, and use as required.

Chasseur Sauce: ½ pint Madère sauce, ½ gill game liquor (fumet), lemon-juice, and 1 to 2 livers of game.

Chop the liver finely and cook with the sauce and liquor of game for about ten minutes, season to taste, add a teaspoonful of lemon-juice and serve.

Chasseur Royal Sauce: 1 small onion, bay-leaf, parsley, thyme, marjoram, 10 peppercorns, 1 glass port wine, ½ pint espagnole sauce, 1 teaspoonful anchovy essence, ½ gill of double cream.

Chop the bones of the fish used, and put in a stewpan with the trimmings of the oysters, the sliced onion, bay-leaf, sprig of parsley and thyme, and a sprig of marjoram.

Moisten with the port wine, let it reduce to half the original quantity. Keep well covered during the process. Now add the crushed peppercorns, anchovy essence, and espagnole sauce, or 1 gill of brown stock. Simmer for twenty minutes, remove the scum, and pass through a tammy cloth or very fine pointed strainer. Return to the stewpan, add a little seasoning if needed, and finish with ½ gill of double cream. Keep very hot, but not boiling, and use as directed.

Châteaubriand Sauce (also called Crapaudine Sauce): 1 gill Chablis or Sauterne wine, 2 cloves, 1 sprig of thyme, 2 shallots, 12 peppercorns, about 1½ gill meat glaze, the juice of ½ lemon, 2 oz. butter, and ½ teaspoonful chopped tarragon.

Peel and chop the shallots, put them with the wine, cloves, thyme, and crushed peppercorns in a small stewpan, cover and reduce to half its quantity, strain into another stewpan, add the lemon-juice. Work in the meat glaze and butter bit by bit (keep the stewpan in the bain-marie), add the tarragon last of all. Whisk well, and serve very hot with fillet steak, Châteaubriand, etc.

Chaud-froid Sauce, Blanche (White Chaud-froid Sauce): ½ pint béchamel or suprême sauce, 1 gill aspic, 5 or 6 leaves French gelatine, 1 gill cream, 1 teaspoonful chili vinegar or lemon-juice.

Dissolve the gelatine along with the aspic jelly, warm up the sauce, and mix the two together. Stir over the fire until it boils, put in vinegar or lemon-juice, and cook for a few minutes. Strain or tammy; add the cream when cooling, and use as required.

Chaud-froid Sauce, Blonde (Fawn Chaud-froid Sauce): ½ pint aspic jelly, 1 gill allemande sauce, ½ gill cream, 1 tablespoonful espagnole sauce, ½ oz. French leaf gelatine, a glass of Madeira wine, pepper and salt.

Melt the aspic jelly in a stewpan, add the wine, espagnole, and allemande sauce, let it come to a boil, and skim. Soak the gelatine in cold water, squeeze it well, and put with the sauce; when dissolved, stir in the cream, pass through a tammy cloth or fine strainer, and use as directed.

Chaud-froid Sauce, Brune (Brown Chaud-froid Sauce): ¼ pint espagnole or salmi sauce, 1 glass Madeira or sherry, ½ pint aspic, 4 leaves French gelatine, and cream.

Boil up the sauce. Dissolve the gelatine with the aspic, mix both together, add the wine, let simmer for a few minutes, and pass through a tammy cloth, add a little cream, and flavor to taste.

Chaud-froid Sauce, Green or Pink: Prepare a white chaud-froid sauce, to which add a few drops of spinach greening to give it a green tint, or a few drops of liquid carmine or cochineal to give it a rose or pink tint.

Chestnut Sauce (Savoury): Par-roast ½ a pound of previously slit chestnuts, and remove the outer skin, then put them in a saucepan of boiling water, and cook until the inner skins can be easily removed. When this is done, stew the chestnuts in seasoned milk till tender, then rub through a sieve. Season to taste with salt and pepper, and dilute the purée with a little rich gravy; reheat, and serve with roast turkey, or as a sauce with grilled and devilled legs of a cold roast bird.

Chestnut Sauce (Savoury or Sweet): Slit a dozen chestnuts and boil them in water, then drain and remove both shell and skin from the chestnuts. Next put them in a saucepan with a glass of claret, and a gill of water, cover, and cook till tender, then rub through a sieve. Re-heat the purée with enough seasoned stock to form a sauce, season with a pinch of cayenne and a grate of nutmeg.

Note: If the sauce is required sweet, use syrup in place of stock, and omit the cayenne.

Venison Sauce (Chevreuil Sauce): ½ pint espagnole sauce, 1 glass port wine, 1 dessert-spoonful red-currant jelly, 1 oz. lean ham, 1 oz. butter, ½ gill vinegar, 1 small onion, 12 pepper-corns, 1 bay-leaf, ½ small carrot, thyme, parsley. Mince finely the onion and ham, fry these in the butter, and add the vinegar, crushed pepper-corns, bay-leaf, minced carrot, and a little thyme and chopped parsley. Cover and boil for ten minutes. Then add the espagnole sauce, port wine, and the red-currant jelly. Cook for ten minutes, skim and strain, season to taste, re-heat, and use as required.

Chutney Sauce: Make a sauce the same as directed for venison sauce, omitting the red cur-rant jelly, and adding instead one heaped-up tablespoonful of mango chutney, which must be chopped up rather finely.

Brown Herb Sauce (Colbert Sauce aux Fines Herbes). 1½ gill espagnole sauce, 1 glass of Madeira wine, 1 tablespoonful of meat glaze, 1½ oz. of fresh butter, 1 teaspoonful lemon-juice, chopped parsley, tarragon, and chervil—one des-sertspoonful in all.

Put the sauce into a small stewpan, stir over the fire until hot, add the wine, and let boil a few minutes. Remove to the side of the stove, and stir in gradually the butter and the meat glaze. Beat up with a small whisk, but do not let it boil again. Last of all add the lemon-juice and the chopped herbs. Serve as directed. If desired richer, ½ oz. more butter may be added in the manner described.

Cream Sauce (Sauce à la Crème): Put into a saucepan the yolks of two eggs, 3 tablespoonfuls of cream, 2 tablespoonfuls of velouté or other rich white sauce, and whisk in half an ounce of fresh butter; season with a pinch of salt and paprika pepper, and lastly add a teaspoonful of lemon juice. Stir or whisk, and cook in a bain marie till it becomes of a creamlike consistency.

Aspic or Savory Cream (Crème à l'Aspic): ½ gill béchamel or allemande sauce, 1 teaspoonful tarragon vinegar, ½ pint aspic jelly, 1 gill double cream, cayenne, mignonette pepper.

Warm up the béchamel or allemande sauce, add the tarragon vinegar, stir this into the liquid aspic jelly, mix with it the cream, season with a pinch of cayenne and mignonette pepper. Pass through a sieve or tammy cloth, and use as directed.

Cold Cucumber Sauce (Sauce aux Concombres): ½ cucumber, ½ gill béchamel sauce, ½ gill cream, 1 gill mayonnaise sauce, salt, pepper to taste, spinach greening.

Peel thinly the cucumber and cut into small pieces, boil in salted water till tender, and rub through a hair sieve. Return the pulp to the stewpan, add the béchamel sauce; let it reduce to about half the original quantity, and let it cool. Whip the cream until stiff; work in the mayonnaise sauce, and mix slowly with the reduced cold sauce, add a little salt and pepper if needed, also a few drops of spinach greening. The sauce is then ready for use.

Cucumber Sauce No. 2 (Sauce aux Concombres): Peel a small or half a large cucumber, cut it into pieces, and boil till tender in salted water or white stock. Drain well, and rub it through a fine sieve. Put the pulp into a small stewpan, and let reduce to half its quantity with a gill of Béchamel sauce; season to taste, strain again, and add to it ⅔ tablespoonful of Mayonnaise sauce, into this stir the cold cucumber purée, and place on the ice. Whip up ½ gill of cream. The sauce is then ready for serving.

Cucumber Sauce, Hot (Sauce aux Concombres, chaude) is made in the same way, by omitting the mayonnaise and adding an extra quantity of hot béchamel sauce. Cook for ten minutes before serving.

Crab Sauce: Remove the meat from a crab and shred it finely, then season with salt and paprika pepper. Put it in a saucepan containing a pint of melted butter sauce, and let it simmer for ten minutes. Serve hot.

Cranberry Sauce: Wash and drain half a pint of cranberries, and cook them in a stewpan with half a pint of water and one ounce of castor sugar; when sufficiently tender, pass them through a fine sieve, then mix with the purée a gill of cooked apple pulp, season to taste, and use when cold.

Cumberland Sauce (a Cold Game Sauce): 2 shallots, 1 orange, 1 lemon, 1 dessertspoonful mustard, ½ gill port wine, ground ginger, 2 tablespoonfuls red-currant jelly, 2 tablespoonfuls vinegar, salt, pepper, cayenne.

Mince the shallots, put them in a stewpan with the thin rinds of the lemon and orange cut into fine Julienne strips. Add half a gill of water and cook for ten minutes, then strain and return to the stewpan, adding the mixed mustard, port wine, a pinch of ground ginger, red-currant jelly, the juice of the lemon and orange, and the vinegar. Season with salt, pepper, and a pinch of cayenne, boil up, strain, and serve cold with any kind of game or ducks. A gill of espagnole sauce added improves this sauce.

Cumberland Sauce No. 2: Cut very thinly the outer rind of an orange, then cut the strips into fine shreds. Put them into a small earthenware saucepan (casserole), pour over half a glass of dry port wine, and place on the side of the stove to get warm, then allow to cool and stir in about a teaspoonful of mixed English mustard, a good pinch of salt, and the strained juice of the orange. Next melt about 2 ounces of red currant jelly and stir into the above. A very small quantity of spice such as cayenne or paprika pepper may be added if liked. This is considered essential by many chefs.

Currie Sauce: Prepare the following: Peel 1 onion, scrape finely 1 small carrot, peel 1 small apple and chop all up very small. Fry these in a saucepan with 1 ounce of butter, then add 1 tablespoonful of curry powder and half a pint of tomato purée or sauce. Season to taste with salt and pepper, then add a good ladle of espagnole sauce. Boil for several minutes, pass through a fine strainer, then add a little chopped gherkin and some finely chopped parsley.

Curry Sauce: Peel and slice a small onion, scrape and slice a small carrot, fry both together in half an ounce of butter; when the onion has acquired a light brown color, add one table-spoonful of mild curry powder and stir for a few seconds. Next add a small peeled and chopped apple, moisten with half a gill of tomato pulp and a gill of brown sauce. Allow to boil for a few minutes. Season to taste, and pass it through a fine strainer. Reheat and stir in last of all a finely chopped pickled gherkin.

Danish Sauce (Sauce Danoise): 2 oz. butter, 1 oz. flour, 1 glass sherry, ½ gill Chablis or Sauterne, 1 pint fish stock, ½ oz. grated Parmesan, 2 teaspoonfuls meat glaze, 1 teaspoonful anchovy essence, 1 gill cream, ½ oz. lobster coral, salt and pepper.

Melt the butter in a stewpan, stir in the flour, let it cook a few minutes without taking color. Moisten with the wine and fish stock. Stir until it boils, then add the anchovy essence, meat glaze, and grated cheese. Season to taste with pepper and salt, let simmer gently for a few minutes, skim and pass through a fine sieve. Return to a clean stewpan and bring to a boil. Work in the cream and lobster coral or lobster butter. Keep hot, but do not let it boil again. Serve with dressed fish—salmon, turbot, soles, or lobster.

Demi-Glace Sauce (Half Glaze Sauce): ¾ pint espagnole sauce, 1½ gill good gravy, pepper. Reduce to a half-glaze espagnole sauce with the gravy from roast veal or beef (strained and free from fat); allow to simmer about fifteen minutes, and season with a pinch of pepper.

Devilled Sauce (Sauce Diable): ½ pint demi-glace sauce, 1 tablespoonful mixed mustard, 1 dessertspoonful Worcester sauce, ½ oz. butter, 2 finely minced shallots, cayenne, parsley.

Fry the shallots in the butter to a golden color, add the demi-glace sauce, mixed mustard, Worcestershire sauce, and a good pinch of cayenne. Stir until it boils, skim and pass through a fine strainer, add a teaspoonful of finely chopped parsley, and serve.

Duchesse Sauce: Take half a pint of richly seasoned meat gravy, thicken it with half an ounce of arrowroot, mixed previously with a little cold water or stock, then add 1 tablespoonful of liquid meat glaze, and a wineglassful of dry white wine and a teaspoonful of red currant jelly. Boil up, simmer for a few minutes, and serve.

Prawn Sauce (Sauce aux Ecrevisses): Proceed the same as for sauce Cardinal and include 12 prawns' heads, which must be cut in quarters and placed into the sauce a few minutes before serving.

Crayfish Sauce (Ecrévisse Sauce): Mix half a pint of Béchamel sauce with a gill of small peeled crayfish tails, and finish the sauce with a little crayfish butter as liaison.

Echalote Sauce (Shallot Sauce): Prepare a brown gravy or demi-glace sauce, add to it some finely minced shallots previously blended in butter, some lemon juice to flavor, and finely chopped parsley.

Epicurienne Sauce: 1 small cucumber, 1 gill mayonnaise, ½ gill cream, 1 tablespoonful tarragon vinegar, ¼ gill aspic jelly, 1 teaspoonful anchovy essence, 1 dessertspoonful chopped gherkins, 1 dessertspoonful chutney, pepper, salt, sugar.

Peel the cucumber, cut it into small pieces, cook till tender in salted water, strain and rub through a fine hair sieve. When cold, stir this purée gradually into the mayonnaise sauce, add the cream, aspic, anchovy essence, the vinegar, and chutney (the latter should previously be rubbed through a sieve); season with pepper and salt and a small pinch of castor sugar; add the chopped gherkins and a few drops of spinach greening to give it a greenish tint. This sauce is especially suitable for asparagus, artichokes, or boiled fish.

Epicure Sauce (Epicurean Sauce): This is a white fish sauce consisting of a rich white sauce, mixed with a little essence of crayfish, finely chopped truffles, chilli vinegar, and cayenne pepper to taste.

Espagnole Sauce (Spanish Sauce): 3 quarts of rich stock, 4 oz. lean veal, 1 bouquet garni, 12 peppercorns, 4 oz. butter, 4 oz. flour (sifted), 4 oz. raw ham or lean bacon, 1 carrot, 1 onion, 2 cloves, ½ pint tomato pulp, 1 gill claret, 1 glass sherry, some mushrooms (fresh or preserved).

This is the chief brown foundation sauce—it forms the basis for a large number of other sauces. It is advisable that particular care and attention be paid to the preparation of this important sauce. The ingredients given will produce about half a gallon of sauce. A smaller quantity can be prepared by reducing the quantities in proportion. It is, however, advisable to have at all times an ample supply of this sauce.

Wash and peel the carrot, turnip, and onion, cut up small and put in a stewpan with the bouquet, peppercorns, cloves, and the veal and ham, both cut into pieces. Add an ounce of butter, and stir over the fire until of a nice light brown color; this forms a true mirepoix. Pour off the fat, moisten the mirepoix with the stock, claret, sherry, and tomato pulp, boil gently for about an hour. Skim occasionally. Meanwhile, prepare a brown roux by melting 3 oz. of butter in a stewpan, stir in the flour, and cook very slowly over a moderate fire, stirring all the while with a wooden spoon until it acquires a chestnut-brown color; or place the stewpan in the oven and let it cook, stirring from time to time to prevent it from burning, and to blend the flour better. Allow the roux to cool a little, pour in gradually the prepared stock, etc., stir over the fire until it boils, let simmer slowly for another hour, skim well, and pass through a tammy cloth or fine sieve. If found too thick, add a little more stock. To prevent a thick crust forming on the top of the sauce, stir occasionally until quite cool. Keep the sauce in a stone vessel or pan until wanted. Be sure and boil up the sauce each day if not used at one time, adding a little stock if necessary.

Essence de Gibier Sauce: This is a brown sauce (demi-glace or Madère) enriched with essence of game.

Tarragon Sauce (Sauce a l'Estragon): This is a thin brown sauce of the demi-glace type flavored with tarragon leaves. It is usually served with poultry or quenelles.

Farmhouse Sauce (Sauce Fermiere): Take half a pint of Espagnole sauce, blend it with finely chopped ham, chopped parsley and capers. This sauce is usually served with game.

Fennel Sauce (Sauce Fenouil): To a pint of well-reduced white sauce (Béchamel or Dutch sauce), add some finely chopped fennel. Mix it well and serve with boiled fish.

Flemish Sauce (Sauce Flamande): Prepare a Dutch sauce flavored with fish stock, then thicken it with yolks of eggs as liaison, and flavor it with a little prepared mustard.

Fleurette Sauce: This is a white sauce, served with fish or vegetables, made with the usual proportions of flour, butter and fleurette (which is the name applied to the first skimming of milk which is rather sweet); season the sauce with salt and pepper to taste.

Financière Sauce: Prepare a rich brown sauce, reduce with sherry or Marsala and mushroom liquor, and enrich it with liquefied meat extract. Thinly sliced truffles, small mushrooms and cock's-combs are added when the sauce is ready for serving.

Game Sauce (Sauce Gibier): Some game bones and trimmings, 1 pint espagnole or brown sauce, ½ gill sherry, onion, carrot, turnip, parsley, thyme, marjoram, bay-leaf, mace, clove.

The trimmings, carcasses, etc., of any kind of game may be used for this sauce; those of grouse or woodcock are preferable. Chop small the trimmings of game, put them in a stewpan with a small onion, a piece of carrot, and a piece of turnip all cut in slices, a few sprigs of parsley, a sprig of thyme, one of marjoram, a bay-leaf, a small piece of mace, and one clove, moisten with the sherry, cover and put on the fire to cook for five minutes. Now add the espagnole or brown sauce, let it come quickly to a boil, and keep simmering for fifteen minutes longer. Pass through a tammy cloth, return to a clean stewpan, season with a little salt if necessary, and keep hot in the bain-marie until required for serving.

Garibaldi Sauce: Prepare a Génoise sauce made with meat or fish basis, flavor it with a suspicion of pounded garlic and curry powder, finely chopped capers, and anchovy essence or paste to which a little chili vinegar should be added, just enough to flavor. Careful blending of the above named flavoring ingredients is essential when making this sauce.

Générale Sauce: This is a rich brown sauce made with a basis of Demi-glace or Madére which is reduced with a small quantity of lemon juice and tarragon vinegar. A little finely shredded orange rind, previously reduced in some sherry, is then added. The sauce is flavored with very little garlic or shallot, bay leaf, clove and mace. Careful blending of the flavoring ingredients is most essential for this sauce.

Génoise Sauce: Melt an ounce of butter in a stewpan, and fry in it a sliced onion, a shallot, half a clove of garlic and a small bouquet garni, add a glass of Burgundy, and let simmer until the onions are done, then add a pint of Espagnole sauce, and let simmer gently for ten minutes. Strain through a fine sieve or tammy, add a pinch of mignonette pepper, and a teaspoonful of anchovy essence, and use as directed.

Genoise Sauce: No. 2. Prepare a mirepoix of 1 carrot, ½ stick of celery, 1 onion, 2 fresh mushrooms, and 2 ozs. bacon, all cut into dice. Melt 1 oz. of butter in a stewpan, add the above mirepoix, also one bay leaf and a few peppercorns, and fry for five minutes over a brisk fire. Add one tablespoonful of flour, stir till it acquires a nut-brown color. Moisten with one glass of Burgundy wine and ½ pint of fish stock. Boil up and simmer for half an hour. Strain, and season to taste. Re-heat and serve as required for fish.

Génoise Sauce (Rich Brown Fish Sauce): 1 sliced onion, 1 shallot, ½ clove of garlic, 1 oz. butter, small bouquet garni, 1 teaspoonful anchovy essence, 1 glass red wine (Burgundy), 1 pint espagnole sauce (made from fish stock if desired), a pinch of mignonette pepper.

Melt the butter in a stewpan, and fry onion, shallot, garlic, and bouquet, add the wine, let simmer until the onions are done, then add the sauce, and let simmer gently for ten minutes. Strain through a fine sieve or tammy, add the pepper and anchovy essence, and use as required.

Giblet Sauce: Boil some previously washed giblets in seasoned water with an onion. When done, strain, take up the giblet and onion, and chop both finely. Put this purée into a saucepan with a piece of butter, add the strained stock and gravy and a small glass of claret; season with aromatics and salt. Simmer slowly for about ten minutes longer, then blend with a little rich brown sauce or roux, re-heat, and serve hot.

Gooseberry Sauce (Sauce aux groseilles vertes): Put half a pound of green gooseberries in a saucepan with a very little water, and cook till soft, then mash them, grate in a little nutmeg, and sweeten with castor sugar to taste. Pass through a sieve and finish with an ounce of butter. Serve with roast pork or roast goose; it is also sometimes served with boiled mackerel. A little spinach greening may be added to the sauce if liked.

Gouffé Sauce: Required: 1 gill cream, ½ gill

wine vinegar, 3 yolks of eggs, 1 bay-leaf, 6 crushed peppercorns, salt, 2 oz. butter, 2 tablespoonfuls of cream, 1 tablespoonful chopped lobster meat.

Put the vinegar, bay-leaf, and peppercorns in a stewpan (covered); let it reduce a little. Add the yolks of eggs and stir over the fire until the sauce begins to thicken, then remove and put in a saucepan containing boiling water, or in the bain-marie. Work in the butter a little at a time, also the cream, stir vigorously with a small whisk. Pass through a fine strainer or tammy cloth, return to a clean stewpan, add the chopped lobster and a pinch of salt, stir again, place a few bits of butter on top, and keep hot until required for serving.

Granville Sauce: Prepare a white wine fish sauce or other rich white sauce, to which add some finely chopped preserved mushrooms (champignons), also a few picked shrimps and finely chopped truffles.

Gravy Without Meat: Cut up into thin slices half a peeled onion and a small scraped carrot, fry both in half an ounce of butter or dripping; when nicely browned add half a pint of water, and a teaspoonful of Marmite or Savoy extract. Boil up, season with salt and pepper, and cook for ten minutes. Skim well, then strain and serve as required.

See also Jus-Gravy.

Green Mousseline Sauce (Sauce Mousseline verte): To half a pint of mayonnaise add a tablespoonful of savory herb purée prepared as follows: Blanch a handful of parsley, tarragon, chervil, and a little fennel, drain, and pound in a mortar with 2 peeled and chopped shallots, a teaspoonful of capers, 2 gherkins, 2 filletted anchovies, 1 hard-boiled yolk of egg, and a tablespoonful of salad oil. Rub through a fine sieve, mix a tablespoonful of tarragon vinegar with half a gill of aspic jelly, whisk all together till frothlike, then stir it into the prepared mayonnaise.

Gribiche Sauce: Take half a pint of Mayonnaise sauce, and add sufficient mixed mustard to flavor, then stir in some finely chopped fresh savory herbs (fines herbes) and serve.

Hâchis Sauce: Mix some well reduced brown sauce with a little rich gravy from roast meat, then add finely chopped mushrooms (champignons), also chopped gherkins and capers in due proportion. Cook a little and serve.

Ham Sauce (Jambon Sauce): Prepare a rich brown sauce, and mix it with finely shredded, grated, or chopped ham, chopped chives, shallots, and parsley, previously blended in butter, then flavor with lemon juice and the necessary seasoning. Boil up and serve hot.

Héssoise Sauce: Prepare a good horse-radish sauce with grated horse-radish, sour cream, and fresh breadcrumbs (previously soaked in milk); season to taste with castor sugar, white pepper, and salt. This sauce is usually served hot.

Hollandaise Sauce (Dutch Sauce): Crush about a dozen peppercorns, put them in a saucepan with 2 tablespoonfuls of French wine vinegar and 4 tablespoonfuls of water. Cover the pan and place it on the fire, boil fast to confuse the contents of the pan. It should be reduced to about one-half its volume. Stir or whisk in 4 yolks of eggs, then by degrees whisk in 4 to 6 oz. of fresh butter, and lastly add about a gill of hot water. Season with salt and the juice of ½ a lemon. Pass the sauce through a fine tammy cloth. Return it to a clean saucepan, which must stand in a pan of hot (not boiling) water. Keep it thus till required for table.

Dutch Sauce (Hollandaise): Take 4 eggs, 4 oz. butter, 4 tablespoonfuls of water, 4 tablespoonfuls of tarragon vinegar, 1 dessertspoonful of flour, and the juice of half a lemon. Mix the butter and the flour together into a paste, put this into a saucepan with the vinegar and water, stir for a few minutes, then add the beaten yolks of the four eggs. Whisk until the mixture thickens or binds, but on no account allow it to boil. When ready to serve add the strained juice of half a lemon. Green Dutch sauce is made by adding a little spinach greening, just sufficient to give it a sage green tint.

Dutch Sauce (Hollandaise Sauce) No. 2: Required: 3 yolks of eggs, 2 oz. butter, 1 gill béchamel sauce, 1 gill stock, the juice of half a lemon, salt and pepper.

Boil up the sauce, remove to the side of the stove and whisk in the yolks of eggs, add the stock (fish, chicken, rabbit or veal), mix thoroughly and add the butter gradually, season with pepper and salt and the lemon-juice. Pass through a tammy and use. Before adding the butter the sauce should be sufficiently heated to bind the eggs. Great care must be taken to prevent curdling. Another way to make this sauce is to omit the béchamel, and to use 4 yolks of eggs to ½ a gill of stock, which is finished with 4 oz. of butter. The first is the most convenient and most popular way. This sauce, when finished, is to be just hot, and on no account must it be allowed to reach the boiling point.

NOTE: A less expensive Hollandaise sauce can be made by adding a small quantity of béchamel or other good white sauce to the above.

Hollandaise Sauce (No. 3) (Inexpensive): Take 2 tablespoonfuls vinegar, 1 shallot, peeled and chopped, 1 bayleaf, 6 white peppercorns crushed, 1 gill white sauce, 2 yolks of eggs, 1 teaspoonful lemon juice, 2 ozs. butter, and salt to taste.

Put the vinegar (French wine vinegar in preference to malt vinegar) with the shallot, bayleaf and peppercorns, in a saucepan, and reduce to half its original quantity; add the white sauce, let it boil, remove the bayleaf and stir in the yolks of eggs. When it begins to thicken, remove from the fire and strain into another saucepan. Re-heat, taking great care that the sauce does not curdle, and whisk in the butter by degrees; lastly add the lemon juice and enough salt to taste. Serve with boiled fish, artichokes, asparagus, etc.

Hollandaise Sauce (No. 4): Put into a jar the yolks of four eggs, 4 ozs. of fresh butter, half a teaspoonful of mignonette pepper, a peeled and chopped shallot, a teaspoonful each of tarragon and chilli vinegar. Put the jar into a stewpan containing boiling water, and stir over the fire till it thickens. Then strain and serve.

Hollandaise Sauce (No. 5): Put one sliced onion, six peppercorns, a bayleaf, into a saucepan with 2 ounces of fresh butter; stir over the fire until the butter is melted, then add a level tablespoonful of flour, fry a little without browning, and stir in gradually ¾ of a pint of white stock, season with a little grated nutmeg and salt, stir until boiling, cook slowly for 10 minutes, then add the yolks of 3 eggs and the juice of half a lemon, stir until it thickens, but do not let it boil again, then strain and serve.

Green Dutch Sauce (Sauce Hollandaise Verte): Mix Hollandaise or Dutch sauce with sufficient young parsley leaves, boiled, drained, pounded, and rubbed through a fine sieve, to impart a green tint. Blend well, reheat and serve hot.

Holstein Sauce: Prepare a white sauce of the Béchamel type, reduce it well with fish stock and white wine, then thicken with a liaison of egg yolks, and flavor with lemon juice and very little nutmeg. Serve hot.

Horly (or Orly) Sauce: Blend Suprène or other rich white sauce with tomato purée and meat extract or liquefied meat glaze, and finish by whisking in fresh butter. Serve hot.

Horseradish Sauce: Grate a stick of washed and scraped horseradish, and put it in a basin with a little lemon juice. Rub the yolks of two hard boiled eggs through a sieve, and mix with about four tablespoonfuls of cream; season with salt and pepper and add a teaspoonful of made mustard and half a gill of vinegar; stir till well blended, then stir in the prepared horseradish, and the sauce will be ready for serving after standing for about two hours.

Horseradish Sauce (No. 2): Grate finely a stick of washed and scraped horseradish. Whip up half a pint of thick cream, and add a tablespoonful of chilli vinegar and a teaspoonful of French or English mustard. Stir in the grated horseradish, mix thoroughly, and serve.

Horseradish Sauce (No. 3): Grate finely two

tablespoonfuls of horseradish after it has been
well washed and scraped, then pound it in a
mortar, add a teaspoonful of salt and half a teaspoonful of castor sugar. Mix it gradually with
a gill of cream, then stir into it quickly half a
gill of vinegar, next add a teaspoonful of made
mustard and a pinch of cayenne or Nepaul
pepper.

**Horse-radish Sauce, hot (Sauce Raifort,
Chaude):** 2 tablespoonfuls grated horse-radish,
½ pint béchamel, ½ teaspoonful castor sugar,
pinch cayenne and salt, ½ teaspoonful vinegar.

Moisten the horse-radish with the vinegar,
mix with the sauce, and boil up whilst stirring.
Add the sugar and cayenne, allow it to simmer
a few minutes, taking great care that the sauce
does not curdle; if found too thick, add a tablespoonful of cream or milk. Served with hot roast
beef, etc.

**Horse-radish Cream, cold (Creme de Raifort,
froide):** 1½ oz. grated horse-radish, 1 gill thick
cream, 1 tablespoonful white wine vinegar, 1
teaspoonful castor sugar, ¼ teaspoonful powdered
mustard, ½ saltspoonful salt, a pinch of cayenne.

Put the horse-radish in a basin, add the sugar,
mustard, salt, and cayenne; moisten with the
vinegar. Stir in gradually the cream, and whisk
gently for a few minutes. Serve in a sauce-
boat with cold roast beef, etc.

**Horse-radish Sauce, Iced (Sauce Raifort frap-
pée):** 1 stick horse-radish, 1 gill cream or milk,
1 teaspoonful mixed mustard, 1 teaspoonful castor sugar, 2 teaspoonfuls vinegar.

Grate the horse-radish as finely as possible,
put it in a basin, stir in the cream or milk, the
vinegar, mustard, and the sugar. Stir well and
pour into a sauce-boat.

When milk is used, a tablespoonful of condensed Swiss milk should be mixed with the
fresh milk, and the sugar should then be omitted.

Freeze till a semi-liquid consistency, serve
with trout or other fish.

Boar's Head Sauce (Sauce Hûre de Sanglier):
Prepare a sauce with Seville orange juice, and
the finely-chopped rind, castor sugar, red-currant

jelly, port wine, and prepared mustard, in due
proportions, then season with salt and black
pepper. Mix well and serve cold. This sauce
is also useful for almost every kind of cold
meat, and will keep for some time if bottled.

Indian Curry Sauce (Sauce Indienne): Required: 1¼ oz. butter, ½ oz. flour, ½ small
onion, 1 tablespoonful curry-powder, ¾ pint good
fish stock, salt, 1 tomato, a few savory herbs,
½ glass sherry or Marsala.

Melt the butter, add the onion, finely chopped;
when of a nice light brown stir in the flour and
curry-powder, blend well, and cook for five minutes; pour in gradually the fish stock, add the
tomato, cut into slices, and the herbs; bring it
to the boil whilst stirring, then add the wine,
season to taste, cook for twenty minutes, strain
and serve.

Italian Sauce (Sauce Italienne): Required:
½ pint Espagnole sauce, 4 small shallots, 8 preserved mushrooms, a sprig of thyme, 1 bay-leaf,
1 tablespoonful sweet oil, 1 glass Chablis or
Sauterne, ½ gill stock.

Peel the shallots, chop them finely, place in
the corner of a clean cloth, hold tightly wrapped
up under cold water, then squeeze out the water,
and put them in a small stewpan with the oil,
stir over the fire for a few minutes, to blend
but not to color. Add the wine, the mushrooms
(finely chopped), herbs, and the stock, let it
reduce well, and add the espagnole. Boil for ten
minutes, take out the herbs, free it from the oil,
and keep hot in the bain-marie until required.

Joinville Sauce: Required: 1 oz. flour, ½
gill fish stock, ¾ pint white stock, 3 oz. butter,
3 yolks of eggs, lobster coral, lemon-juice, salt,
and cayenne.

Melt 1 oz. of butter in a saucepan, stir in the
flour, and cook a little without browning. Add
gradually the fish and white stock, stir until it
boils, and let simmer for twenty minutes. Pound
the lobster coral in a mortar with an equal
quantity of fresh butter, rub through a sieve
and stir into the sauce. Stir in the egg-yolks
one at a time. Season to taste with a pinch of

cayenne, salt and lemon-juice. Whisk well over
a slow fire, or in a bain-marie. Do not let the
sauce boil up again. Pass through a fine-pointed
strainer or napkin, and serve as directed.

Joinville Sauce (No. 2): Knead an ounce of
butter with an ounce of sifted flour in a stewpan,
put it in the hot stove and stir for a few minutes, so as to cook the flour (be careful not to
let the flour get brown). Add the liquor from
the fillets, and about half a pint of white stock,
stir until it boils, and let simmer for about 10
minutes. Remove the scum, stir in 2 more
ounces of butter and 2 yolks of eggs. Season
with white pepper and salt, add a few drops of
lemon juice and sufficient lobster-spawn to give
the sauce a pinkish tint, but do not on any account let the sauce boil again. Stir it long
enough over the fire so as to bind the liaison.
Pass the sauce through a fine strainer or tammy
cloth, and use same as directed.

Jus (Brown Gravy): Required: 2 oz. beef
suet or 1 oz. dripping, 2 lb. trimmings of meat,
1 onion, 1 carrot, ½ head celery, 2 cloves, 1
blade mace, 6 peppercorns, bouquet of herbs, 2
quarts water.

Put the beef suet or dripping in a stewpan,
add a sliced onion and carrot, fry till brown,
put in the beef trimmings or other meat, and
any bones of meat or carcass of poultry. Let it
bake in the oven for fifteen minutes, take up,
pour off the fat, and moisten with the water.
Add the celery, cloves, mace, peppercorns, and
bouquet of herbs. Let the whole simmer gently
for several hours, take off fat and scum, and
strain. Season with salt as required. A few
drops of caramel may be added if the gravy is
not sufficiently brown.

Karl Sauce: This is a mild kind of curry
sauce composed of white sauce flavored with
curry and cream.

Lemon Sauce (Sauce au Citron): Melt an
ounce of butter in a stewpan, stir in half-ounce
flour and half-ounce of cornflour; cook a little
without browning, and gradually stir in half-
pint milk; add the thin rind of half a lemon;

cook whilst stirring for ten minutes. Dilute
with a little stock (and this may be fish, vegetable, meat or chicken stock, according to the
dish with which it is served), adding the juice
of half a lemon at the same time. Season with
pepper and salt, cook for another five minutes.

NOTE: The yolk of an egg and a little cream
may, if liked, be added to this sauce.

Livournaise Sauce: This is a cold salad sauce
of the Vinaigrette type, prepared with pounded
anchovy fillets, hard-boiled yolks of eggs, sweet
oil, vinegar, chopped parsley, pepper, and nutmeg. All ingredients must be used in due proportions and be well blended before the sauce is
served.

Lobster Sauce (Sauce Homard): Take half a
pint of béchamel sauce, add to it two heaped-up
tablespoonfuls of finely chopped lobster, including a little coral or spawn; mix, and heat up
carefully whilst stirring; season with a pinch of
cayenne or paprika pepper, and serve when hot.

Lobster Sauce (No. 2): Slit a small hen lobster, take out the coral, and crack the claws,
then remove all the flesh and cut it into very
small pieces or dice. Pound the coral in a mortar
with half an ounce of butter, and rub through a
fine sieve. Melt in a stewpan 1 ounce of butter
and add about ¾ of an ounce of flour, blend all
well together, then add a gill of water and a gill
of milk, and stir this mixture over the fire until
it boils and thickens; cook it for about ten minutes, then strain and reheat, now add a little
cream, and stir well until it boils again, then
whisk in, by degrees, whilst off the fire, the coral
butter, stir till it is quite smooth, season with
salt, pepper and a pinch of cayenne, put in the
chopped lobster last of all to the sauce, mix well,
and finish with a little lemon juice.

Lyonnaise Sauce: Mix a well made tomato
sauce with finely cut small shreds of Spanish
onions (previously fried in butter); finish the
sauce with a little liquefied meat glaze and lemon
juice and serve hot.

Madeira Sauce (Madère Sauce): Proceed the
same as for Demi-glace. Add one glass of sherry

or Marsala; reduce a little longer than the above, and finish with a little meat glaze.

Maintenon Sauce: Blend about a gill of white onion purée (Soubise type) with two or three egg-yolks and half a pint of hot Veloutée sauce; reheat, season to taste with salt and white pepper, and serve hot.

Maintenon Sauce: No. 2. This sauce is especially adapted for so-called gratin dishes, and must therefore be well reduced to the correct consistency. 1 pint Béchamel sauce, 4 yolks of eggs, 1 tablespoonful Parmesan cheese, 1 tablespoonful cooked onion purée, garlic, paprika pepper, nutmeg.

Boil the Béchamel sauce for about fifteen minutes, stirring continually; add to it the yolks of eggs, Parmesan cheese, cooked onion purée (Soubise), a suspicion of garlic, just enough to impart the aroma, a pinch of paprika pepper, and a little grated nutmeg (salt if needed). Stir till it thickens, without allowing it to boil, and use as required.

Parsley or Fine Herb Sauce (Maître d'Hôtel Sauce): ½ pint Béchamel or Velouté sauce, 3 oz. butter, ½ lemon, 1 teaspoonful of chopped parsley seasoning.

Put the sauce into a stewpan, add a little water, stir until it boils, and reduce well. Whisk in the butter a little at a time, and rub through a tammy cloth or fine hair sieve. Return to the stewpan, add the parsley and lemon-juice, season with pepper and salt.

Maître d'Hôtel Sauce (No. 2): Warm up 1 pint of béchamel sauce, add to it a tablespoonful of finely chopped parsley, a few chervil and tarragon leaves, and a tablespoonful of lemon juice; work up with an ounce of fresh butter, and serve hot.

Malaga Sauce: Take some good brown sauce, enrich it with liquefied meat glaze, then blend it with port wine and lemon juice, reduce well, season with cayenne and flavor with finely chopped and previously fried shallots. Serve hot.

Maltaise Sauce: Dilute and reduce finely chopped parsley, shallots and mushrooms with sherry, and blend with Veloutée or Allemande sauce, then flavor with lemon juice and add finely shredded orange rind.

Marchand de Vin Sauce (Wine Merchant Sauce): Peel and chop finely 3 shallots, toss these, i. e. blend in a stewpan containing half an ounce of butter, then pour in a gill of claret, cover, and reduce a little. Next add half a pint of Demi-glace or Espagnole sauce, a small piece of meat glaze, and enough salt and pepper to taste. Boil up whilst stirring, skim, and let simmer for a few minutes. Lastly stir in half a pat of fresh butter, and about a teaspoonful of lemon juice. This sauce is usually served with grilled steak or fillets of beef.

Marguéry Sauce: Take some white fish sauce (of the Mornay type), blend it with oyster purée, season to taste with salt and white pepper, and finish with a little double cream.

Marinade Sauce: Cut a large carrot and two peeled onions in slices, and fry these vegetables in oil with a bay-leaf, a sprig of thyme, a clove of garlic, a sprig of parsley, two chopped shallots, and a little crushed pepper. When they are fried without taking a brown color, moisten with a mixture of vinegar and water, adding a little salt. Allow to simmer for twenty minutes, then strain and repeat with a pint of Espagnole sauce.

Marinade Sauce No. 2: ½ pint stock, ½ gill vinegar, 1 tablespoonful flour, 1 oz. butter, 1 small carrot, 3 shallots, thyme, 1 clove, parsley, bayleaf, chives, flour.

Melt the butter in a stewpan, add the sliced carrot, sliced shallots, a sprig of thyme, and the clove. Fry a little, then add a few sprigs of parsley, a bay-leaf, some chives, and a tablespoonful of flour. Stir over the fire for a few minutes. Moisten with the vinegar and stock, season with pepper and salt. Allow to simmer for half an hour, strain or pass through a tammy cloth, and serve as required for relevés, roast or braised game, etc.

Marinière Sauce: Mix some white wine sauce with finely chopped herbs and shallots previously blended in butter, and enrich with a little fish essence.

Matelote Sauce: ½ pint of espagnole sauce, 1 oz. butter, ½ gill Burgundy wine, ¼ gill fish stock, liquor or fumet, ½ onion, ½ carrot, ½ gill mushroom liquor.

Peel the onion and carrot and mince very fine, fry in a little butter a nice color, drain off the butter, moisten with the wine and mushroom liquor, let this reduce well, then add the fish stock or liquor and the espagnole. Let simmer for ten minutes; then strain through a fine strainer or cloth, add a small piece of butter, season, if necessary, with a few drops of lemon-juice, salt and pepper, and keep hot.

NOTE: When Espagnole is not handy, substitute for it ½ oz. of flour, ½ oz. of butter, well blended (fried to a chestnut brown), and diluted with ½ pint of rich brown stock; boil well, skim, season, and strain.

Matelote Blanche Sauce: Blend a white sauce with mushroom liquor, white wine, and finely chopped peeled button mushrooms previously blended in butter. Cook well. Strain, reheat, and add chopped oysters flavored with chopped savory herbs and very little anchovy essence.

Matelote Brune Sauce: Blend a red wine sauce (Génoise, or Merchant de Vin) with finely chopped fried button onions and button mushrooms, used in due proportion; flavor with chopped savory herbs and very little anchovy essence.

Marseillaise Sauce: ½ lb. ripe tomatoes, ½ carrot, 1 small onion, 1 oz. raw ham, 2 oz. butter, 1 oz. flour, 1 bay-leaf, 1 pint chicken-stock, 1 oz. bacon (fat), and salt, pepper to taste.

Remove the stems of the tomatoes, cut them in halves, crossways, take out the pips and mash up, and put them in a stewpan with the stock and vegetables; the latter should be washed, peeled, and cut into slices. Cook slowly until tender. Cut up the bacon and ham, put them in a stewpan with 1 oz. of butter, stir over the fire for five minutes; add the flour, and cook long enough to blend the flour (do not let it get brown); now add the tomato purée, the bay-leaf, the stock, and the chicken. Allow to cook together slowly for twenty minutes. Season with pepper, salt, and a pinch of aromatic seasoning. Pass through a tammy cloth or hair sieve, heat up again, and whisk in the rest of the butter.

Maximilian Sauce: Prepare a Tartare sauce and blend it with sufficient tomato pulp or purée to give it a reddish tint, then add sufficient finely chopped tarragon leaves to flavor. Serve cold.

Mayonnaise Sauce: 2 yolks of eggs, 1 teaspoonful of French mustard, ½ teaspoonful salt, a pinch of pepper, 1 tablespoonful of tarragon vinegar, about ¾ pint best salad oil, and 1 tablespoonful of cream.

Put the yolks into a basin, add the mustard (raw, not mixed), salt and pepper; stir quickly with a wooden spoon, adding, drop by drop at first and gradually more, the salad oil, and at intervals a few drops of vinegar; the vinegar is added when the sauce appears too thick. By stirring well, the mixture should become the consistency of very thick cream. At last add the raw cream, stirring all the while. A little cold water may be added if found too thick. In hot weather the basin in which the mayonnaise is made should be placed in a vessel of crushed ice.

Mayonnaise Sauce (No. 2): Put two yolks of eggs into a clean basin, add a heaped up saltspoonful of salt, and stir with a wooden spoon, adding little by little (drop by drop) one and a half gills of best salad oil, and at intervals a tablespoonful of French wine vinegar. Continue to stir vigorously till the mixture acquires a creamy substance, then add another tablespoonful of vinegar, a teaspoonful of mixed mustard, and lastly a few drops of chilli vinegar, and use as required.

Mayonnaise Sauce (No. 3): Break the yolks of 2 eggs into a mixing basin, add a pinch of castor sugar, half a teaspoonful of salt, and a saltspoonful of mustard. Stir with a wooden spoon till smooth, then add drop by drop half a pint of good olive oil, stirring briskly all the time. Great care must be taken in adding the oil, otherwise it will curdle. Then add a dessertspoonful each of tarragon and chilli vinegar, and finally 2 tablespoonfuls of whipped cream.

Mayonnaise Sauce tomatée: To a pint of well prepared and fairly stiff mayonnaise add half as much tomato purée or cold tomato sauce. Mix gradually, and season to taste.

Medicis Sauce: Blend a nicely prepared Béarnaise sauce with tomato purée previously diluted and reduced with a little red wine. Serve hot.

Melted Butter Sauce: 1 oz. fresh butter, ¾ oz. flour, and ½ pint cold water.

Put the butter in a saucepan, when melted stir in the flour (sifted). Cook for a few moments whilst stirring, add gradually ½ pint of cold water, continue to stir till the sauce boils, and allow to cook for at least ten minutes. Add salt and pepper to taste, and strain if necessary.

Mint Sauce (Sauce à la Menthe): 2 tablespoonfuls finely chopped green mint, 1 dessertspoonful brown sugar, 3 to 4 tablespoonfuls vinegar.

Put the mint into a basin, add the sugar and pour over a little warm water, sufficient to dissolve the sugar, cover and let cool, then add the vinegar, stir well, and pour into a sauce-boat.

Mint Sauce (No. 2): Wash a small bunch of green mint in cold water, then strip off the leaves from the stems, and chop them finely. Put them in a small basin, with 1½ gills of good vinegar and a little moist sugar; stir well, and serve when required. The correct proportion of mint and sugar to the above quantity of vinegar is two tablespoonfuls of chopped mint and one small dessertspoonful of moist or Demerara sugar.

Mint Sauce (No. 3): Wash and drain a small bunch of green mint, sprinkle over it a good pinch of salt, chop it finely, and add to every tablespoonful of chopped mint one tablespoonful of water, one of white wine vinegar, and a teaspoonful of castor sugar. Mix well and serve.

NOTE: A pinch of borax added to this sauce is considered by some cooks an improvement.

Mirabeau Sauce: 1 gill espagnole sauce, 1½ gill fish stock, ½ small onion, ½ small carrot, ¼ gill Burgundy wine, ¼ gill mushroom liquor, 1½ oz. fresh butter, chopped tarragon, chervil, and parsley.

Prepare the fish stock from the bones and trimmings from fresh fish. Peel the onion, scrape the carrot, and mince both; fry them in a little butter to a nice color, drain off the butter, add the wine, cover and let boil quickly for a few minutes. Add the mushroom liquor and the stock, reduce to about half the original quantity, then stir in the espagnole sauce, and let simmer for about five minutes. Strain into a clean saucepan, add the remainder of the butter, about a teaspoonful (in all) of chopped parsley, tarragon, and chervil, also a few drops of lemon-juice and seasoning if found necessary. Whisk over the fire until thoroughly hot (not boiling), and use as directed.

Miroton Sauce: Blend some Demi-glace sauce with finely minced, blanched and fried onions, and tomato sauce, add vinegar and mustard to taste, reduce well, season with salt and pepper, and serve hot.

Mornay Sauce: Required: ½ pint Béchamel sauce, ½ gill mushroom or Italienne sauce, ½ gill cream, ½ oz. meat glaze or 2 tablespoonfuls half-glaze of chicken stock, ½ oz. grated Parmesan cheese, and 1 oz. fresh butter.

Put the Béchamel sauce into a saucepan, reduce it well, then add the Italian or mushroom sauce. Let it boil up, skim well, and add the cream. Place the stewpan in a vessel of boiling water, stir the sauce with a whisk, adding the grated cheese, butter, and meat glaze; work in these ingredients little by little, and stir or whisk till the sauce has acquired a creamy texture. Do not allow the sauce to boil again. This sauce is usually served with fish—in which case a little fish essence should also be incorporated before serving.

Mousseline Sauce (White): Required: ½ gill cream, 4 yolks of eggs, 3 crushed long peppercorns, 1 oz. butter, salt, nutmeg, lemon-juice.

Put the cream, egg-yolks, and pepper in a stewpan, place this in a bain-marie half filled with boiling water, beat up with a whisk for a little time, then add gradually little pieces of butter, stirring all the while, but do not add any more butter until each piece has been thoroughly worked in and is absorbed in the sauce. The sauce when finished will have the appearance of a frothy cream, and should then be passed through a tammy cloth. Just before serving finish off with a few drops of lemon-juice, a pinch of salt, and a grate of nutmeg should be added during the process of whisking. Served with soufflé, fillets of veal or fowl, asparagus or artichokes.

Mousseline Sauce Verte (Green Mousseline Sauce, cold): Required: 1 gill mayonnaise, ½ gill cold Béchamel sauce, 1 tablespoonful of pickled parsley, a few sprigs each of tarragon, chervil, and burnet, 2 tablespoonfuls of cooked spinach, 2 hard-boiled yolks of eggs, 2 anchovy fillets, and ½ gill of cream.

Wash and pick the green herbs, steep them in boiling water for a few minutes, drain well, pound in a mortar with the spinach, and rub through a fine sieve. Pound the yolks of eggs and anchovy fillets, mix with the green purée, add the cream, and rub the whole through a sieve. Dilute with mayonnaise and Béchamel sauce, add a little seasoning and a teaspoonful of mixed mustard.

Mustard Sauce (Sauce Moutarde) (for grilled or boiled Herrings or Mackerel): 1 oz. butter, ½ oz. patent cornflour, ¼ oz. flour, 1 dessertspoonful of English mustard, ¼ gill vinegar, ¼ pint fish stock, ½ gill cream, pepper and salt to taste.

Melt the butter in a small saucepan, stir in the cornflour and flour, and blend over the fire without browning. Add the fish stock and bring it to the boil, cook for ten minutes. Mix the mustard with enough vinegar to make a smooth paste, stir this into the sauce with the cream, boil up again. Season to taste with pepper and salt, and add a little more vinegar just before serving.

Mussel Sauce (Sauce aux Moules): Mix some Hollandaise or Dutch sauce with cooked mussels cut into small dice, season to taste and serve hot.

Nantua Sauce: Heat up 1½ gills of Béchamel sauce, and stir in ¼ gill of cream, then finish with ½ oz. of crayfish butter. Crayfish tails may if liked be mixed with this sauce just before serving.

Niçoise Sauce: Blend some Demi-glace sauce with a small quantity of concentrated Italian tomato purée, season to taste and serve hot.

Nonpareille Sauce: Prepare a Hollandaise or Dutch sauce, and incorporate some crayfish or lobster butter, then add finely chopped lobster meat, preserved mushrooms (champignons), hard-boiled whites of eggs, and truffles, all in due proportions and finely chopped. Serve hot.

Normande Sauce: 2½ oz. butter, 1 oz. flour, white stock, fish liquor, 2 yolks of eggs, and lemon-juice.

Melt 1½ oz. of butter in a stewpan, add the flour, stir long enough to cook the flour, moisten with about a pint of white stock and a little fish liquor. Allow to boil for ten minutes, skim well, and finish with a liaison of 2 yolks of eggs. Stir in gradually the remainder of the fresh butter, and a few drops of lemon-juice. Whisk well and pass the sauce through a fine strainer or tammy cloth.

Norvégienne Sauce: Prepare a cold sauce of the Mayonnaise type with hard-boiled egg yolks previously passed through a sieve, yolks of fresh eggs, salt, pepper, made mustard, oil and vinegar, then mix in some finely chopped savory herbs. Serve cold.

Noisette Sauce (Nut Sauce): Take some Hollandaise or Dutch sauce and blend it with previously baked, pounded and sieved hazel nuts. Finish the sauce by whisking in a little cream.

Egg Sauce (Sauce aux Oeufs): To a pint of white sauce (Béchamel or Melted Butter) add 1 to 2 hard-boiled eggs chopped up small. Season to taste with salt and pepper and serve hot.

Egg Sauce (Sauce aux œufs durs): Boil an egg for ten minutes, place it in cold water and remove the shell. Separate the yolk from the white and chop each finely. Mix with half a pint of white sauce or béchamel, previously heated, season to taste, heat up.

Onion Sauce (Sauce aux Oignons): 2 onions, 1 oz. butter, ½ oz. flour, ½ pint milk, nutmeg.

Peel the onions, cut them in halves and blanch them, drain and cook in salted water till tender, drain again and chop finely. Melt the butter in a saucepan, stir in the flour, cook a little and add gradually the milk; stir till it boils and put in the chopped onions, season with pepper and a grate of nutmeg, and cook for 10 minutes longer.

NOTE: When brown onion sauce is required, mince the onions and fry a light brown color in butter, drain off the butter and add half a pint of brown sauce, cook for 15 minutes.

Onion Sauce (No. 2): Take some white sauce in which a due proportion of finely chopped boiled onions have been cooked; season with salt, nutmeg and pepper. Served with boiled rabbit or boiled or baked mutton.

For brown onion sauce, the onions are first fried in butter and then cooked in Demi-glace or Poivrade sauce.

Olive Sauce: Make a good brown sauce, mix it with stoned or turned French olives, season to taste and flavor with a little lemon juice. Serve hot.

Orange Sauce (Sauce à l'Orange): 2 peeled shallots, 1 orange, lemon-juice, 2 ozs. raw ham, cayenne to taste, 2 glasses port wine, and 1 gill of meat gravy.

Chop the shallots and put them into a small stewpan with the rind of the orange, quite free from the white or pith, and a little chopped lean of raw ham and cayenne pepper; moisten with the port wine, and a little meat gravy; set the essence to simmer gently on the fire for about ten minutes, then add the juice of the orange with a little lemon-juice, and pass it through a silk sieve.

Orange Sauce (No. 2): (For wild duck, wild fowl, widgeon, teal, etc.) Mix half a gill of rich brown sauce with a gill of meat gravy, to this add the strained juice of an orange, and boil up; skim, and season with salt and pepper. Shred finely the rind of half an orange, and put it into the sauce, boil up again, and serve.

NOTE: If liked, a small, finely chopped shallot and half a glass of port wine or claret can be added and cooked with the above sauce. This is considered an improvement.

Jus d'Orange Sauce: ½ pint Espagnole sauce, ½ pint good stock or gravy, 1 orange, lemon-juice, and 1 teaspoonful red-currant jelly.

Peel the orange thinly, and cut the peel into Julienne strips, put them in a stewpan with sufficient water to cover, boil for five minutes, and drain on a sieve. Put in a stewpan, the Espagnole sauce, stock or roast meat gravy, and half the juice of the orange. Allow all to reduce to half its quantity, strain, and add the orange-peel, a teaspoonful of lemon-juice, the red-currant jelly, season with pepper and salt, boil up again, and serve with roast wild duck, wild boar or other game.

Sorrel Sauce (Oseille Sauce): Prepare a thin gravy sauce or use Demi-glace sauce; to which add finely chopped and blanched sorrel leaves. This sauce is usually served with braised or boiled fowls, etc.

Oyster Sauce (Sauce aux Huîtres): Required: 12 oysters, 1 oz. of butter, a teaspoonful of lemon-juice, 1 yolk of egg, and ¾ of a pint of béchamel sauce.

Open the oysters, remove the beards and put them, with their liquor, in a small saucepan, with the butter. Cover with the lid, and cook for four minutes (they must not be allowed to boil). Put the oysters on a sieve, cut them in halves or quarters, allow the liquid to reduce to half its original quantity. Strain, return to the saucepan, add the béchamel sauce; when hot bind with the yolk of egg, then put in the oysters and lemon-juice. Stir till quite hot, but do not let it boil. Season to taste and serve.

Oyster Sauce (Sauce aux Huîtres): Reduce half a pint of Béchamel sauce with the strained liquor of six sauce oysters. Beard the oysters and cut them into quarters, or smaller, if liked; boil for a few seconds only, then season with a few drops of lemon-juice and additional salt and pepper, if found necessary.

Oyster sauce forms an excellent adjunct with boiled fish—especially so with turbot and cod, also with boiled poultry, such as fowl or turkey.

Paprika Sauce: This consists of Veloutée or Allemande sauce highly seasoned with paprika, which is Red Hungarian pepper.

Parisienne Sauce: This is a rich brown sauce flavored with previously blended chopped shallots to which add some finely chopped parsley, a little lemon juice and some liquefied meat glaze, then finish by whisking in a little fresh butter. Serve with entrecôtes, steaks or fillets of beef.

Parsley Sauce (Sauce Persil): Prepare half a pint of Béchamel or other white sauce, to this add 1 dessertspoonful of finely chopped and washed parsley and a few drops of lemon-juice.

Pekoe Sauce: Mix 2 ounces of butter and a teaspoonful of English mustard into a paste, then season with salt and pepper and a tablespoonful of Worcestershire sauce. Put this into a stewpan and let it gradually get hot. This sauce is excellent with red mullet.

Pérsillade Sauce: Prepare a Vinaigrette sauce in the usual manner with olive oil, vinegar, salt, pepper, lemon juice and made mustard, then stir in some finely chopped parsley and green savory herbs. This sauce is usually served cold with fish, vegetables, or as a salad dressing.

Périgueux Sauce (Truffle Sauce): 1 gill brown sauce, 1 gill tomato sauce, 1 glass sherry, 1 teaspoonful anchovy essence, 1 oz. butter, 3 truffles.

Chop finely three large truffles, put them in a small stewpan with the sherry, reduce to one-half (covered); add the brown and tomato sauce; boil for a few minutes, finish with a teaspoonful of anchovy essence and the butter.

Piment Sauce: Take some Demi-glace sauce and blend it with tomato purée, to which add some finely chopped pimento or sweet pepper and season sparingly with cayenne. Serve hot.

Piquante Sauce (Sharp Sauce): ½ onion or 4 shallots, 3 gherkins (chopped), 1 tablespoonful chopped capers, 1 gill vinegar, ½ teaspoonful anchovy essence, 1 bay-leaf, 1 sprig of thyme, and ¾ pint espagnole sauce.

Peel and chop the onion or shallots, put them in a stewpan with the vinegar, bay-leaf, and thyme, cover, and reduce to half the quantity of liquor. Strain into another stewpan, add the chopped gherkins and capers, moisten with the sauce, add the anchovy essence, boil a few minutes, and serve.

Piquante Sauce (Another Method): Chop separately four shallots, three pickled gherkins, a tablespoonful of piccalilly, and a dessertspoonful of French capers. Put in a stewpan with a bay-leaf, a sprig of thyme, and a gill of French wine vinegar; cover the stewpan and let reduce to half the quantity. Remove the herbs, dilute with a pint of Espagnole sauce, season with pepper, boil up and skim.

Piquante Sauce (No. 3): Take half a small onion or 2 shallots, 2 chopped gherkins, 1 tablespoonful chopped capers, 1 gill vinegar, 1 bay-leaf, 1 sprig of thyme, and ½ pint Espagnole or brown sauce.

Peel and chop finely the onion or shallots, put them in a stewpan with the vinegar, bay-leaf, and thyme, cover and reduce to half the quantity of liquor. Strain into another stewpan.

Piquante Tartare Sauce. Required: 1 gill of olive oil, 2 yolks of eggs, 1 tablespoonful of gherkins, 1 tablespoonful of French vinegar, 1 tablespoonful of tarragon vinegar, 1 teaspoonful of made mustard, 1 teaspoonful of anchovy essence, salt and cayenne.

Put the yolks of egg in a mixing bowl, place this if possible on ice or in very cold water, next add the oil drop by drop, stirring or whisking always in the same direction, until the eggs become thick, then add vinegar to taste and other ingredients. The gherkins should be chopped finely and added separately to the anchovy essence; all this must be carefully mixed together. Keep in a cool place until needed.

Poivrade Sauce (Pepper Sauce): ¾ pint of Espagnole sauce, ½ oz. of butter, ½ small carrot, ½ small onion, 18 peppercorns. 1 bay-leaf, 1 sprig thyme, 2 cloves, and ½ oz. of raw ham or bacon.

Mince the onion and carrot, cut the ham or bacon into small pieces; fry the above in the butter for three minutes, add the peppercorns (crushed) herbs, etc., skim off the fat, moisten with the sauce, and boil for ten minutes or longer; skim, season, strain, and serve as required.

Polish Sauce (Polonaise Sauce): Take ½ pint of Veloutée sauce and blend it with a little sour cream, some finely grated horseradish, and finely chopped fennel, and flavor with lemon juice. Serve hot.

Pompadour Sauce: 2 oz. butter, ½ pint veloutée or allemande sauce, 1 shallot, 6 preserved mushrooms, 2 yolks of eggs, ¼ gill cream, 1 teaspoonful chopped parsley, pepper, salt and a grate of nutmeg.

Peel and chop the shallot, and mince finely the mushrooms. Blend the shallot in an ounce of butter, but do not let it take color; put in the mushrooms and stir over the fire until all moisture is absorbed, then add the sauce, stir until it boils, skim well, and let it cook a few minutes. Beat up the yolks of eggs with the cream and parsley, stir into the sauce and season with pepper, salt and a little nutmeg; finish with the remaining ounce of butter, but do not let it boil again. Keep in the bain-marie until required for serving.

Pauvre Homme Sauce (Poor Man's Sauce): Prepare a plain brown sauce, to which add sufficient tomato ketchup and anchovy fish essence to flavor. Suitable as a fish sauce to be served hot.

Portugaise Sauce: Reduce about a pint of tomato sauce with a gill of rich veal gravy, flavor it with finely chopped onion, blanched and fried in butter, with a little crushed garlic.

Poulette Sauce: Melt an ounce of butter and stir in ¾ ounce of flour, cook for a few minutes

without browning the flour, then stir in 1 pint
of white stock, stir till it boils, and cook for at
least 15 minutes, thicken with 2 yolks of eggs,
season with salt and pepper, and finish with half
an ounce of fresh butter.

**Prince of Wales Sauce (Prince de Galles
Sauce):** This is a cold sauce prepared with
chopped yolks of hard-boiled eggs and yolks of
raw eggs, olive oil, tarragon vinegar, mixed with
finely chopped savory herbs, and prepared French
mustard. It is usually served with grilled or
fried fish, or grilled meats à la Tartare.

**Princesse Sauce (Hot Sauce for Fried Chicken,
etc.):** 1½ gill of Béchamel or veloutée sauce,
2 tablespoonfuls French wine vinegar, 1 oz.
fresh butter, 1 lemon, 1 teaspoonful of grated
horse-radish, nutmeg, 8 pepper-corns and parsley.

Put the grated rind of the lemon and the horse-
radish in a small stewpan with the French wine
vinegar, add a little grated nutmeg and the
crushed white peppercorns, boil for several minutes, then add the Béchamel or veloutée sauce.
Cook for ten minutes, and pass through a fine
sieve or tammy. Re-heat, season with salt and
more pepper, if needed, work in by means of a
whisk the butter and a teaspoonful of finely
chopped parsley, and serve with any kind of
fixture of poultry, fish or meat.

Provençale Sauce: Put two tablespoonfuls each
of finely chopped preserved mushrooms and
peeled shallots, two cloves of crushed garlic, and
a small bunch of sweet savory herbs into a saucepan, and pour over a gill of olive oil; season
with salt and pepper. Cook steadily with the lid
on, shaking or stirring frequently, and then add
1 pint of brown sauce (Espagnole) and a wineglassful of white wine. Simmer for about half
an hour, then take out the bunch of herbs, and
serve.

Demi-Provençale Sauce: This is practically the
same as the above, omitting the mushrooms, shallot, herbs and wine, and adding half a teaspoonful of castor sugar. Strain the sauce before
serving.

Ravigote Sauce, Chaud (Hot Ravigote Sauce):
Take some hot Béchamel sauce, and blend it with
finely chopped, green, savory herbs, previously
reduced with white wine vinegar, then finish the
sauce with a liaison of butter and cream, season
to taste, and serve.

Ravigote Sauce, Froid (Cold Ravigote Sauce):
Take some Mayonnaise sauce, mix it with sufficient finely chopped parsley, chives, chervil, tarragon, and peeled shallots, then stir in a little
spinach greening to give it the necessary color.

Réforme Sauce (for Cutlets à la Réforme):
1 gill poivrade sauce, 1 small glass port wine,
1 teaspoonful red-currant jelly.

This sauce consists of poivrade sauce mixed
with port wine and red-currant jelly. Boil well
for ten minutes, and strain. The usual Reform
garnish, consisting of Julienne strips of gherkins, mushrooms, truffles, hard-boiled white of
egg and cooked ox-tongue, is served at the same
time.

Régence Sauce (Regent Sauce): Blend ½ pint
of Demi-glace sauce with ½ pint of thin gravy
sauce, and reduce both with a little white wine
and truffle essence, then flavor with finely minced
and butter blended onions.

Rémoulade Sauce: ½ pint salad oil, 2 tablespoonfuls tarragon vinegar, 1 teaspoonful made
mustard, tarragon, parsley, burnet, chives, 1
yolk of egg, castor sugar.

Blanch a few leaves of tarragon, parsley, burnet, and chives, drain and chop finely. Put in
a basin the yolk of egg with salt and pepper to
taste, stir well with a wooden spoon, work in
gradually half a pint of salad oil, and at intervals a few drops of tarragon vinegar. About
two tablespoonfuls of vinegar is required to
half a pint of oil. When the sauce is finished
add a teaspoonful of made mustard, a pinch of
castor sugar, and the chopped herbs.

Rémoulade Sauce (No. 2): Blanch a few leaves
of tarragon, fennel, parsley, burnet, and chives;
drain the herbs, and chop them very finely. Put
in a basin the yolk of an egg, with salt and
pepper to taste; stir well with a wooden spoon.

Work in gradually half a pint of salad oil, and at intervals a few drops of tarragon vinegar. About two tablespoonfuls of vinegar are required to half a pint of oil. When the sauce is finished, add a teaspoonful of made mustard, a pinch of castor sugar, and the chopped herbs.

Ricardo Sauce: Prepare a fumêt from the carcase of game, to which add finely minced fried onions and toasted bread, and blend with rich brown sauce, strain, flavor with sherry, and finish with a little liquefied meat glaze.

Riche Sauce: This is Hollandaise enriched with lobster butter or spawn, to which small dice shapes of truffle and crayfish tails are added just before serving.

Richelieu Sauce: This is a rich brown game sauce, reduced with Madeira or Marsala wine, then work in a little liquefied meat extract and some finely chopped truffles.

Robert Sauce: ½ small onion, ½ oz. butter, ½ teaspoonful castor sugar, ½ pint Espagnole sauce, ½ glass white wine, and saltspoonful dry mustard.

Peel and mince the onion, fry it in the butter a nut brown, add the mustard, moisten with the wine, and reduce a little. Stir in the Espagnole and cook for ten minutes; season it to taste, and strain.

Roman Sauce (Romaine Sauce): Take a pint of Espagnole sauce, heat it up, and mix with a small quantity of each, cleaned currants, sultanas and Italian pine seeds, then reduce with a little white wine vinegar; press all through a sieve, reheat, season and serve.

Royal Sauce: Put an ounce of butter into a stewpan, when melted stir into it a heaped up dessertspoonful of flour, add gradually ½ pint of fish stock, stir till it boils, and let simmer for about 10 minutes. Strain, reheat, and add a tablespoonful of cream, a teaspoonful of anchovy essence, and a tablespoonful of "Pan Yan" sauce. Season to taste, reheat without boiling, and serve with boiled turbot or salmon.

Rouennaise Sauce: 2 shallots, bay-leaf, a

sprig of thyme, 1 glass claret, 1 pint demi-glace sauce, and 2 or 3 ducks' livers.

Infuse the finely chopped shallots, bay-leaf, and a sprig of thyme in the glass of claret. Add the demi-glace sauce and the finely chopped ducks' livers, and let reduce, season to taste, and strain.

Russian Sauce (Sauce Russe): Chop finely 2 oz. of lean ham, 4 peeled shallots, and fry in butter (about ½ oz.) for a few seconds, then add a bay-leaf, a sprig of thyme, and a glass of white wine; cover, and let reduce to about half the quantity. To this add about a pint of veloutée or allemande sauce, and allow to cook gently for ten minutes. Remove the herbs, and add a tablespoonful of finely grated horse-radish, season with cayenne and nutmeg, and pass through a seive or tammy cloth. Re-heat, stir in a pat of fresh butter, and a teaspoonful of liquified meat glaze. This sauce is excellent with grilled fish or fillets of beef.

Cold Salmon Sauce: Take 4 ounces of butter, one tablespoonful of anchovy essence, two tablespoonfuls of chilli vinegar, one tablespoonful of cold water, a grate of nutmeg and a pinch of salt. Put all into a mixing basin to warm and stir or whisk till quite smooth, then stir in the yolk of an egg, mix well, and serve when quite cold.

Salmi, or Salmy Sauce: Required: 1 teaspoonful red-currant jelly, ½ pint Espagnole sauce, 1 gill of game stock, carcass of cooked game, 2 shallots, 1 bay-leaf, a sprig of thyme, some mushroom trimmings, 1 glass port wine, 1 tablespoonful sweet oil.

Peel and chop finely the shallots, fry in oil a golden color, add the bay-leaf, thyme and mushroom trimmings, chop up the carcass of game, and fry a little in fat or butter, drain, and put with the above preparation, add the port wine, cover the stewpan, and cook them for five minutes. Moisten with the stock and sauce. Stir well and let simmer for ten minutes. Skim well, strain or tammy, season to taste, add the red currant jelly, heat up and serve.

Seville Sauce: Reduce some Demi-glace sauce with strained orange juice and add the finely chopped rind of a Seville orange. This sauce is usually served with roast or braised ducks or game.

Sharp Sauce: Peel and chop a small onion. Heat up in a saucepan 2 tablespoonfuls of salad oil and fry in it the onion to a golden color, then add an ounce of flour and let brown nicely; next put in 1 teaspoonful of crushed peppercorns, 3 preserved mushrooms and a tomato (cut up small); add gradually a pint of stock, and stir until the mixture boils, then add 2 tablespoonfuls of vinegar and a few savory herbs. Simmer at least 15 minutes longer, then strain; re-heat, skim, season to taste with salt and pepper, including a tiny pinch of cayenne, and serve hot.

Shrimp Sauce (Sauce aux crevettes): ½ pint white fish sauce, ¼ pint picked shrimps, vinegar, 1 teaspoonful anchovy essence, 1 small blade of mace, 1 bay-leaf.

Boil the shells and heads of the shrimps in enough vinegar to cover; to this add a small blade of mace and a bay-leaf. Strain the liquor into the sauce, add the picked shrimps, and boil up. Finish with a teaspoonful of anchovy essence, and serve with boiled or grilled fish.

Shrimp Sauce (No. 2): Take 1 pint of milk, 1½ ozs. of butter, 1 oz. flour, ½ pint of shrimps.

Pick the shrimps, and put the skins into the milk, allow this to boil, and then strain. Melt the butter, stir in the flour, cook a little and add the milk gradually; keep stirring till it boils and cook for ten minutes. Add the shrimps just before serving, and if liked a few drops of essence of anchovy.

Sicilienne Sauce: Reduce some Espagnole sauce with Marsala or Sherry, season sparingly with cayenne pepper; add some thinly cut rings of onions fried in butter just before serving.

Soubise Sauce: 2 onions, 1 gill white stock, ½ pint Béchamel sauce, white pepper, salt, a pinch sugar.

Peel the onions, parboil in salted water, strain,

drain, and chop very finely. Return to the stew-pan, and stir over the fire until all moisture is absorbed, then add the stock and cook till tender. Now add the sauce and reduce to the desired consistency, season with pepper, salt, and a pinch of castor sugar.

Soubise Sauce No. 3: Peel, slice and blanch 3 onions, then cook them in half a pint of milk, half an ounce of butter, a little pepper and salt, a bunch of herbs, thyme, parsley and bayleaf, and half a pint of wine sauce. Boil slowly for about 20 minutes, then remove the herbs, and pass the onions and sauce through a fine sieve. Reheat the sauce in a bain-marie, and stir in two tablespoonfuls of cream just before serving.

Soubise Tomato Sauce: Peel and slice a large Spanish onion, and cook it in white stock or sea-soned water until tender, and the liquid has nearly evaporated, then rub all through a fine sieve. Add one-half the quantity of hot cream, and an equal quantity of hot tomato sauce; sea-son with salt and pepper to taste. Reheat the sauce, but do not let it boil again.

Soyer Sauce: Prepare a white fish sauce or Béchamel "Maigre," and flavor it with finely chopped savory herbs, butter blended shallots and lemon juice. Finish the sauce with a liaison of egg yolks and cream.

Spadacini Sauce Required: 1 gill white wine, ½ gill vinegar, 2 shallots, a few sprigs of pars-ley, 2 sprigs of basil, 1 teaspoonful crushed mig-nonette pepper, 1 tablespoonful white sauce—Béchamel or allemande, 1 tablespoonful tomato sauce, 1 small terrine foie-gras (about 3 oz.) freed from fat, 1 yolk of egg, 1 oz. butter, and 2 pinches of cayenne.

Put the wine, vinegar, shallot (chopped finely) herbs, and peppercorns in a stewpan, cover, and reduce to one half of its original quantity. Add the two kinds of sauces, boil up, and pass through the tammy. Pound the foie-gras in a mortar, add the yolk of egg and the butter. Rub this through a sieve and incorporate, in small quantities, with the sauce. Whisk the sauce en bain-marie whilst this is being done. Season with a pinch of cayenne, and use as directed. The sauce must not be allowed to boil, and when finished should be similar in consistency to Béarnaise.

Stragotte Sauce: This is a rich brown game sauce with the addition of tomato pulp and madeira wine, flavored with celery purée and parsley roots, shallots, cloves and mace. This sauce is generally served with Italian dishes.

Suprême Sauce: 1 oz. butter, 1 oz. flour, 1 pint chicken stock, 1 small onion, 1 clove, ½ bay-leaf, 3 oz. fresh butter, 1 tablespoonful cream, 1 yolk of egg, ½ lemon.

Make a white roux with the butter and flour, and dilute with the chicken stock. Boil up, add the onion, clove, half bay-leaf, and let it simmer for fifteen minutes. Skim well, and work in the butter, cream, yolk of egg, and the juice of half a lemon. Whisk well, and pass through a tammy cloth.

Suprême Sauce (No. 2): Put an ounce of butter in a stewpan; when melted, stir in an ounce of flour; allow it to cook a little. Add gradually a pint of well seasoned chicken stock, stir until it boils, and allow to simmer for fifteen minutes. Take off the scum, add a gill of cream, a teaspoonful of lemon juice, a pinch of salt, and a pinch of grated nutmeg. Pass through a tammy cloth or napkin, return to a clean stewpan, and finish with half an ounce of fresh butter and a little chicken essence or veal glaze.

Swedish Sauce (Sauce Suedoise—Hot): Make a Béchamel or other white sauce, flavor it with grated horse-radish and chilli vinegar, and serve with roast poultry or grilled meats.

Swedish Sauce (Cold): 1 gill mayonnaise, ¼ gill cream, 1 teaspoonful of French mustard, and 2 tablespoonfuls finely grated horse-radish.

Whip the cream, stir in gradually the mayonnaise, grated horse-radish, and mustard; add a pinch of castor sugar, and a little salt if needed.

This sauce is especially suitable for salads and served with roast game, etc.

Tartare Sauce: 2 yolks of eggs, cayenne, mustard, 1 pint salad oil, ¼ gill tarragon vinegar, Béchamel or veloutée sauce, 2 tablespoonfuls chopped gherkins, 1 tablespoonful of chopped capers, 1 tablespoonful of chopped parsley, ½ teaspoonful of mixed tarragon and chervil finely chopped.

Put the yolks of eggs in a basin, place it in a shallow pan containing some crushed ice, add a teaspoonful of salt, a good pinch of white pepper, a pinch of cayenne, and a teaspoonful of mustard; stir well together, and add, gradually, the salad oil and tarragon vinegar. When the sauce is smooth and creamy stir in a good tablespoonful of cold Béchamel or veloutée sauce, add the gherkins, capers, parsley, tarragon, and chervil. Do not mix the gherkins, capers, etc., until the sauce is finished, as it is likely to cause the sauce to turn if put in too soon. A few drops of lemon juice may be added if the sauce is found too thick.

Texas Sauce (Sauce Texienne): Prepare a curry sauce, mix it with a very little saffron and finely chopped parsley, flavor with lemon juice, and finish with a liaison of fresh butter and cream.

Tomato Sauce (Sauce Tomate): 1½ pint stock, 1 oz. streaky bacon, 1 oz. butter, 1 small onion finely chopped, 1 lb. tomatoes, 1 oz. flour, peppercorns, herbs, parsley, 1 oz. fresh butter, castor sugar.

Put into a stewpan the butter and onion, fry a little, and add the tomatoes cut into slices. Stir over the fire a little longer, then add the flour previously mixed with a little cold stock or gravy. Stir the stock in gradually, add a few peppercorns, a few sprigs of savory herbs and parsley, and allow all to simmer for half an hour. Remove the herbs, rub the sauce through a sieve, return to the stewpan, season with salt, a pinch of castor sugar and pepper, whisk the butter, and serve as required. A tablespoonful of cream can be used instead of butter, but the sauce should not be allowed to boil again after the butter or cream has been added.

Tomato Sauce (No. 2): Cut half a pound of ripe tomatoes into slices, also half a small peeled onion, and cook them for about 20 minutes with a teaspoonful of castor sugar, a few peppercorns, half a bayleaf and half a teaspoonful of salt. Rub through a sieve or strainer, and add a pint of brown stock. Fry in an ounce of butter ¾ ounce of flour, and stir until well browned, then pour in gradually whilst stirring, the hot tomato liquid. Boil up, skim, and let simmer for about 15 minutes, then serve.

Tomato Cream Sauce (Sauce Crème à la Tomate): 2 oz. butter, 1 large tomato, 1 bay-leaf, 6 peppercorns.

Cut up the tomato, put in a stewpan, add the bay-leaf, salt, and peppercorns, reduce to half, add a piece of butter, and when drawn pass through a tammy. Return to a small stewpan, and work in remainder of the butter. Do not put near too hot a place or else it will go oily.

Tortue Sauce (Turtle Sauce): Prepare a rich brown sauce, using turtle stock as a basis, and blend with finely chopped shallots, a little anchovy paste or essence, lemon juice and sherry, reduce and add finely chopped or grated lemon rind, season with very little cayenne pepper, and serve.

Valentine Sauce: This sauce is prepared in the same way as Suédoise Sauce, adding a teaspoonful of tarragon vinegar and substituting the French mustard with half that quantity of English mustard.

Valoise Sauce: Chop finely 3 to 4 peeled shallots, and reduce with a glass of white wine, then add some meat extract or liquefied meat glaze, work in 2 ounces of fresh butter, 3 to 4 egg yolks, and last of all a liaison of cream. Season with salt and pepper to taste, and add some finely chopped parsley, also about a tablespoonful of Worcestershire sauce. Whisk in a bainmarie pan until quite warm, then serve.

Veloutée Sauce (Velvet Sauce): 1 oz. flour, 2 oz. butter, 1 pint of veal stock, ¼ gill mushroom liquor, ½ gill of cream, 1 small bouquet garni, 6 peppercorns, salt, nutmeg, lemon juice.

Cook the flour with an ounce of butter together without browning, stir in the stock and mushroom liquor, add the bouquet and crushed peppercorns, boil slowly for twenty minutes, stir frequently, and skim. Pass through a sieve or tammy keep on the side of the stove, put a few tiny pieces of butter on top to keep from forming a skin. Just before using it add the cream. Stir well and let it get thoroughly hot without boiling, season with salt if necessary, a pinch of nutmeg, and about a teaspoonful of lemon juice. The sauce is now ready for use, and will serve as a foundation for any white sauce or as a veloutée by itself. The cream may be omitted if used as a foundation sauce.

Venison Sauce: Put into a saucepan half a pint of good brown sauce, a dessertspoonful of red currant jelly, half a glass of port wine and the juice of half a lemon. Boil up and season with salt and pepper. Next add a dessertspoonful of meat glaze, boil up again, then skim, strain and serve.

Vénitienne Sauce: ½ pint allemande or Béchamel sauce, 1 oz. lobster butter, 1 dessertspoonful meat glaze, the juice of half a lemon, pepper, nutmeg, and salt, 1 teaspoonful finely chopped tarragon leaves.

Heat up the sauce, stir in the lobster butter and meat glaze when required for serving, add lemon juice, sufficient pepper, grated nutmeg, and salt to taste, and, last of all, the chopped tarragon.

Vert-Pré Sauce (Green Herb Sauce): 2 shallots, 3 oz. butter, 2 large tablespoonfuls white-wine vinegar, ½ pint veloutée (see above) or allemande sauce, a small handful spinach, 6 sprigs of parsley, 2 to 3 sprigs chives, 3 sprigs tarragon, very little chervil, salt and pepper.

Peel and chop finely the shallots, put them in a stewpan with the vinegar and 1 oz. of butter, cover with the lid of the stewpan, and allow to reduce to about half its original quantity. Now add the white sauce (veloutée for preference) and let simmer for a few minutes. Wash, pick, and blanch (parboil) the spinach and remainder

of herbs; drain and cool, press out all the water,
and pound in a mortar with about 1 oz. of butter. Rub this through a fine sieve, and mix it
with the sauce as above prepared. Whisk in
the remainder of the butter, season to taste, and
serve.

Verte glacée Sauce (Iced Green Sauce): 1 me-
dium-sized cucumber, a few sprigs chervil and
tarragon (blanched), spinach greening, 1 dessertspoonful Orléans vinegar, 1 gill aspic, 1 gill
cream, 1½ gill mayonnaise, a pinch of castor
sugar, salt and pepper to taste.

Peel thinly the cucumber, cut it in half, remove the seed portion, then slice, and cook in
slightly salted water till tender. Strain off the
water and rub the cucumber through a fine sieve.
Chop finely the herbs, and add this and the vinegar, with a little spinach greening, to the cucumber purée. Whisk the cream a little, and stir
in the above when sufficiently cool. Incorporate
by degrees the mayonnaise and the aspic jelly
(previously dissolved, but not hot). Stir over
the ice with a whisk for a few minutes, season
to taste, and fill up an oblong biscuit-tin; seal
it with paper and lid, and place it in a charged
ice-cave for 1½ hour. To serve, unmold as
usual, cut the shape into neat slices or cubes,
and serve with grilled fish or meat, etc.

Villeroi Sauce: Prepare a Béchamel or other
rich white sauce, and mix it with finely chopped
cooked ham or tongue or both, and finish with a
liaison of yolks of eggs and fresh butter or
cream.

Vin Blanc Sauce (White Wine Sauce): ½ pint
white stock, ½ gill chablis or sauterne, ¾ oz.
flour, 2 oz. butter, 2 yolks of eggs, ½ lemon,
salt, white pepper, some fish liquor if the sauce
be used for fish.

Melt 1 oz. butter, stir in the flour, cook a little,
dilute with seasoned stock, fish liquor, and wine;
boil up and cook for fifteen minutes. Add gradually the remainder of the butter bit by bit, also
the yolks of egg, one at a time, season with a
little salt, a pinch of mignonette or white pepper,
and add a few drops of lemon juice. Strain

through a tammy cloth, and use as sauce for
dressed fish, etc. Mostly served with soles,
salmon, trout, and whiting.

White Wine Sauce (Sauce au Vin blanc): Put
2 ounces of butter into a saucepan with a little
parsley, a small peeled, sliced and blanched onion,
one or two preserved mushrooms (champignons),
previously tossed in a little lemon juice, all
finely minced; toss them in a stewpan well over
the fire, but do not let them get brown, add an
ounce of flour, add a pint of stock and a glass of
chablis or sauterne; season with salt, pepper and
mace; boil up, skim and simmer gently for about
half an hour, skim, strain and serve.

Vinaigrette Sauce: 3 tablespoonfuls tarragon
vinegar, 1 teaspoonful made mustard, olive oil,
1 teaspoonful chopped gherkins, 1 teaspoonful
chopped capers, ½ teaspoonful chopped parsley,
½ teaspoonful chopped shallots.

Mix in a basin the tarragon vinegar, mustard
(French or English), and ½ teaspoonful of salt.
To this add 6 or 8 tablespoonfuls of best olive
oil, the parsley, shallots, gherkins and capers.
Mix well before serving.

Victoria Sauce (for Fish): ½ lb. fresh butter,
4 yolks of eggs, 1 teaspoonful tarragon vinegar, 1
tablespoonful lemon juice, 1 teaspoonful chilli
vinegar, ½ gill fish stock, ½ oz. lobster butter,
pepper, salt, and nutmeg.

Cut the butter into small squares, put half
the quantity in a stewpan, place the stewpan in
a vessel or large stewpan containing boiling
water. Stir in the yolks of eggs by means of
a whisk, add lemon juice, tarragon, and chilli
vinegar, also the stock reduced to half its quantity. Season with pepper, salt, and a pinch of
grated nutmeg. Finish by whisking in the remainder of the pieces of fresh and the lobster
butter. The water in which the stewpan is
placed should be kept at boiling point during
the process, but on no account must the sauce be
allowed to boil.

Wargrave Sauce: Mix or blend with a pint of
Demi-glaze or other rich brown sauce a dessertspoonful of red currant jelly, a tablespoonful

each of Worcestershire sauce, mushroom ketchup, and tomato purée. When well mixed stir in about a tablespoonful each of the following: pickled gherkins, preserved mushrooms, cooked ham and tongue, all cut into very fine Julienne strips or thin shreds.

Watercress Sauce (Sauce Ruisseau): ½ bunch watercress, ½ tablespoonful capers, 1½ oz. of butter, 1 gill chicken stock, ½ pint veloutée sauce or allemande, 1 hard-boiled egg, seasoning.

Wash, pick, and blanch the cresses, put them in the mortar with the egg, capers, and butter, pound until fine, and rub through a sieve. Put the sauce and stock in a stewpan, let it boil up together, skim, and reduce a little. Whisk in, by degrees, the green purée. Season to taste with pepper and salt, strain through a tammy cloth, return to the stewpan, and keep hot in a bain-marie until required for serving. Do not allow the sauce to boil again after it has been strained, or else it will become oily.

White Sauce (Sauce blanche): Dissolve an ounce of butter in a sauce pan, add one ounce of flour; stir over the fire for a few minutes, just long enough to cook the flour, without allowing to brown. Stir in a pint of boiling milk; add a small onion stuck with a clove, ten white peppercorns, half a bay-leaf, a sliced carrot, a pinch of salt, and a little grated nutmeg. Stir until it boils, and allow to simmer for about fifteen minutes. Pass through a sieve or tammy cloth or else a fine strainer, and return to the stewpan. Lastly stir in with a small piece of fresh butter, and half a teaspoonful of lemon juice.

White Sauce (Simple): 1 oz. butter, 1 oz. flour, ½ pint milk, ½ gill white stock or water, ½ bay-leaf, salt and white pepper.

Melt the butter in a small saucepan, stir in the flour, and cook for a few minutes without allowing the flour to brown; dilute with the milk, stir till it boils, then add the stock and bay-leaf, and let simmer for at least ten minutes. Remove the bay-leaf, season to taste, and strain.

White Fish Sauce: 1 oz. butter, ½ oz. flour, 1 gill milk, 2 tablespoonfuls cream, 1 small piece of mace, ½ bay-leaf, ½ teaspoonful lemon juice, salt and pepper, bones and trimmings of fish.

Boil the milk with some fish-bones, bay-leaf, and a tiny piece of mace, together with ½ gill of water. Melt the butter in a stewpan, add the flour, and stir a few moments over the fire without allowing the flour to take color. Stir about a gill of milk as above prepared into this, allow it to come to the boil whilst stirring, and let simmer for ten minutes; take out the bay-leaf and mace and strain, heat up again, add the cream, lemon juice, and seasoning, and use as directed.

Xavier Sauce (Fish Sauce): ½ bunch watercress, a few sprigs of fennel, ¾ pint milk, fish-bones, essence of fish for which the sauce is prepared, 1½ oz. butter, ½ oz. flour, seasoning, lemon juice.

Remove the stalks from the cress and fennel, put the leaves in a stewpan with the milk and fish-bones, previously cut into small pieces (add a tiny piece of soda), boil until the leaves are done. Strain and let cool, put the cooked herbs in a mortar, and pound with half the butter, then rub through a sieve. Cook the flour in the remainder of the butter, without taking color, dilute with the milk in which the cress, etc., have boiled. Stir until it boils, add the fish essence, and let the whole simmer for ten minutes. Strain, return to the stewpan, boil up, add the green purée, and cook a few minutes longer. Season with a few drops of lemon juice, pepper, and salt, add a little cream or stock if found too thick, and keep in the bain-marie until required.

Yorkshire Sauce (Sauce York): Heat up some Espagnole sauce, then add finely shredded or grated orange rind, red currant jelly, port wine, orange juice, and a little ground cinnamon (careful blending of these ingredients is essential), reduce well and season to taste with salt and pepper. The sauce is served with boiled ham or pickled pork.

Zingara Sauce: Reduce half a gill port wine with a gill tomato purée, add a gill "Salmi sauce," and reduce with half a gill of rich stock; then strain on to a stewpan, containing finely-shredded ham, tongue, mushrooms, and truffles, about 1 dessertspoonful of each, and a few very fine shreds of orange rind. Boil up for about five minutes and serve.

SALAD SAUCES.

Mayonnaise: Of all the cold sauces used either with meat or fish or to season salads the best known, the most popular, and the most agreeable to the palate is without doubt Mayonnaise. Spanish sauce is the fundamental type of brown sauces; velouté is the prototype of white sauces, and Mayonnaise is the sauce from which the cold sauces are derived. Phileas Gilbert in one of his chronicles says: "Mayonnaise is the planet around which numerous satellites gravitate, the highway from which many paths run off." The ingredients which enter into the composition of Mayonnaise properly so-called are few in number, easily manipulated, and successful preparation is simple enough if certain conditions are observed, otherwise the result is disastrous. The first of these rules is to use first-class ingredients, especially the oil, which is the soul of the sauce. The vinegar also must be the best possible, and a good brand of mustard chosen. As for the pepper it should be ground immediately before use. The Mayonnaise of course takes the color of the chopped herbs that are used to season it; thus with a little chervil and tarragon it becomes "sauce verte" (green sauce); with chopped truffles it is "la sauce demi-deuil" (half mourning); it takes the name of "sauce Cardinale" when lobster coral is added, and it is called Portuguese when mixed with tomato; and "indienne" when some curry is put into it. The simple Mayonnaise, however, consists merely of oil, vinegar, pepper, and salt, a little mustard, and the yolk of an egg. There has been much

argument as to how the name Mayonnaise came
to be given to this sauce. One version is that it
is a corruption of Bayonnaise, from the town of
Bayonne, where it originated. Another version
is that the name is really "Mahonnaise," and to
have been given in honor of Marshal Richelieu
after the taking of Port Mahon, the capital of
Minorca, which the Duke made himself master
of after having beaten the English. Another
version attributes the invention of this sauce to
Mayenne, and insists that the name was originally "Mayennaise." Carême says that we
ought to say "Magnonnaise," and that it comes
from the verb "manier" from the energetic stirring the sauce undergoes in course of preparation.
He contradicts this himself in another chapter of
his book, where, in enumerating a list of dishes
named after the localities where they originated,
he cites the word "Magnonnaise" as being derived from the town of Magnon, although at the
same time there is no such town in France. The
philologists dispute every point except that the
sauce is most stimulating, the most unctuous, and
the most appetizing of all cold sauces.

Plain Mayonnaise: The making of a Mayonnaise is the terror of unskilled cooks. To believe
them, there are all sorts of difficulties in making
it. The work is long and troublesome, and the
success of the result is always problematic. Some
pretend that it can only be made over ice, and
that the sauce must always be stirred the same
way. (Both these are gross errors.) It is preferable to operate in the warmth rather than in
complete cold, as the oil in congealing is an
obstacle in the assimilation of the liquid with
the yolk and vinegar and the sauce rapidly
decomposes.

As for the belief that the spoon or whisk
should be turned one way rather than the other,
it is too ridiculous to trouble ourselves with. The
recipe herewith may be considered infallible, not
only because the ingredients are different to those
ordinarily employed, but because of the method
of operating and mixing the ingredients.

Put into a round bowl the yolks of two eggs,

half a teaspoonful of salt, half this quantity of white pepper, a teaspoonful of mustard, and the same of vinegar. Mix these ingredients vigorously with a small metal whisk, add the oil gradually without stopping stirring. Great care must be taken not to allow the Mayonnaise to become too thick. This can be avoided by adding a few drops of vinegar or cold water. The method of mixing the yolks with the mustard, vinegar, salt, and pepper to begin with is the main point of the recipe, and the reason why success is certain, as the mixture assimilates easily with the oil, and it is not even necessary to add it drop by drop, but it may be put in spoonful by spoonful without fear. The principal advantage of the method of operating is that sufficient Mayonnaise for six people can be prepared in five minutes, whereas the old way would take a quarter of an hour. The use of a whisk in place of a wooden spoon is of great importance.

Green Mayonnaise: Take a large sprig of parsley, one of chervil, chives, and tarragon. Wash, blanch, drain, and refreshen. Squeeze out the moisture in a napkin, and put them into a mortar with the yolks of three hard eggs, salt, pepper, two anchovies, and a little mustard. Pound, adding oil and vinegar until the purée becomes smooth. Then pass it through a hair sieve by the aid of a palet knife. Mix this purée with Mayonnaise.

Tomato Mayonnaise: Put the yolks of 2 raw eggs into a mixing basin, add a pinch of salt, and stir in gradually a gill of salad oil. Mix a teaspoonful of tarragon vinegar and one of chilli vinegar, with the same quantity of French vinegar. Work this in by degrees until the sauce assumes a rich creamy consistency. Mix about a gill of tomato purée with the Mayonnaise, and place it on the ice for about an hour, then serve with cold meat or use for a cold entrée.

Mayonnaise aux Fines Herbes: Prepare a Mayonnaise with two egg yolks, and when it is made and seasoned add a little tarragon, chervil, and parsley, all finely chopped. Mix well and serve.

Mayonnaise à la Portugaise: All sauces called Portugaise are usually red, and colored by means of tomatoes. Add to the Mayonnaise a tablespoonful of tomato pulp previously passed through a fine sieve. Mix well and serve.

Mayonnaise à la Cardinale: This sauce takes its name from the scarlet color communicated to Mayonnaise by the addition of crayfish or lobster coral. Pass the coral through a hair sieve, mix with the sauce, and season with a little cayenne or paprika.

Caper Mayonnaise: Mix a tablespoonful or two of finely chopped capers to half a pint of Mayonnaise.

Truffle Mayonnaise: This is a Mayonnaise to which finely chopped truffles have been added. This preparation is known as demi-deuil sauce.

Mayonnaise à la Gelée: Put into a basin some almost cold aspic jelly. Mix this with the same quantity of olive oil and three tablespoonfuls of vinegar. Add a teaspoonful of chopped fine herbs, salt, and pepper. Stir the sauce on ice with an egg whisk until it commences to thicken. Then take it off the ice and whisk it a few minutes longer. This Mayonnaise is usually employed with cold fish or fowl. It is lighter than Mayonnaise made with egg, but is less appreciated.

Cumberland Sauce: This sauce is much in favor in England, and is served with cold game or galantine of boar's head. Chop up two shallots and put them into a stewpan with the juice of an orange and a lemon cut into fine Julienne. Boil in water for twenty minutes and drain. Then put the juice and shallots into a basin with six spoonfuls of currant jelly, three of port wine, a pinch of ground ginger, a little cayenne, and the juice of the lemon and orange.

Sauce à la Diable: This sauce is served and eaten with grilled meat. Chop three peeled shallots and half a clove of garlic, and boil in a small pan with two spoonfuls of vinegar and a sprinkling of cayenne for ten minutes. Add a little tomato sauce and Worcester sauce, and allow to cool. Mix this with a rather thick Mayonnaise.

Pepper Sauce: Pepper sauce properly so-called is served hot with certain entrées, and usually with braised fillet of beef, but the cold pepper sauce eaten with artichokes and asparagus is simply made with oil, vinegar, pepper, and salt, to which a little mustard may be added.

Ravigote Sauce: The name of ravigote was formerly given to a mixture of herbs chopped finely, composed of parsley, chervil, tarragon, chives, pimpernel, and capers. This is the origin of ravigote sauce, which is a simple vinaigrette seasoned with these herbs and with the addition of chopped or pounded yolk of hard-boiled egg. This sauce, in the old days, was known as "grebiche."

Rémoulade Sauce: Rémoulade is often confounded with ravigote, although the sauces are entirely different. Rémoulade differs from other cold sauces insomuch as mustard is its characteristic basis, and it is flavored with pounded anchovies. Chop up finely three shallots and fry them in oil, stirring them until they take a light color. Then drain and let them cool. Chop up some parsley, chervil, and pimpernel. Put these herbs in the corner of a napkin, and steep them in boiling water. Press out the moisture by wringing the linen, and put the herbs into a bowl with the chopped shallot, two teaspoonfuls of tarragon mustard, salt, and pepper. Add oil drop by drop, stirring with a wooden spoon or with an egg whisk, and finally put in a sufficient quantity of vinegar. Add the oil to the mustard very carefully, otherwise the sauce will decompose.

Rémoulade Sauce à l'Indienne: Pound in a small mortar the yolks of four hard-boiled eggs, adding ½ pint of oil and ⅛ gill of vinegar, drop by drop. Add two teaspoonfuls of curry paste, season, and pass through a sieve. This is used with poultry or game salads. It should have a very pronounced yellow color.

Tartare Sauce: Mix the yolks of three hard-boiled eggs in a small basin, then add a teaspoonful of French mustard and as much English mustard. Season with salt, pepper, and a spoonful of vinegar. Mix with an egg whisk and allow the oil to run from the bottle in a thin thread, whisking constantly until the sauce thickens. It can be thinned with vinegar if necessary. Add finally capers, chopped gherkins, chervil, tarragon, and a sprinkling of cayenne. If these instructions are followed to the letter the sauce should not turn. Either hard-boiled or raw yolks of eggs may be used.

Vinaigrette: This is usually served with asparagus and globe artichokes. It should not be prepared in advance. As a rule each person makes it on his own plate. It is simply composed of oil, vinegar, salt and pepper, to which a little mustard may be added; chopped parsley, gherkins, etc., can also be mixed with it if liked.

FRUIT SAUCES.

The continental custom of serving fruit sauces as an accompaniment with certain fish, roast, braised or boiled meat, roast game and poultry is becoming fashionable in other countries.

Apple Sauce (served with roast pork, goose, or duck): Peel and core 1 lb. of cooking apples and slice thinly, put them into a stewpan with an ounce of sugar, and a teacupful of cold water. Cook the apples until they are tender and will mash easily; they require from three-quarters of an hour to an hour to cook. Pass the fruit through a wire sieve, return the sauce to the stewpan, stir in about an ounce of butter, and serve hot.

Apple Sauce (Another Way): Peel, core and slice 6 large sour cooking apples and cook them till tender with ½ pint rich gravy, rub through a fine wire sieve and add a tiny pinch of cayenne.

Brown Apple Sauce: Peel, core and slice thinly about 1 lb. of cooking apples, put them in a stewpan with about a pint of brown stock or gravy, and let them boil until the fruit is tender. Stir them and mash them from time to time, and when they are mashed add half a saltspoonful of cayenne pepper. Serve hot.

Cherry Sauce (Served with Roast Snipe and Woodcocks): Remove the stems from ½ lb. of cooking cherries, stone them, wash them and drain them from the water into a stewpan, add an ounce of sugar and the juice of half a lemon. Let the cherries stew gently for three-quarters of an hour. Serve them hot in a sauce boat.

Cranberry Sauce (Served with Roast Turkey, Duck or Game): Wash ½ lb. of cranberries, then put them in a stewpan, add sufficient water to cover them, and an ounce of sugar. Allow the cranberries to stew for about half an hour, and serve when cold.

Damson Sauce: To a pint of vinegar add a pound of loaf sugar, half an ounce of cloves, and 3 quarts of damsons. Boil all together till the fruit is tender, then pass through a fine sieve, and bottle and cork at once.

Gooseberry Sauce (Served with Mackerel and Roast Pork, and Sometimes with Boiled Lamb or Mutton): Top and tail a pint of green, unripe gooseberries, wash them, and place them in a stewpan, add an ounce of sugar, a gill of cold water. Cover the stewpan and cook slowly for about half an hour; shake the pan from time to time to prevent the fruit from sticking. When the fruit is quite soft, pass through a sieve, and serve the sauce hot.

Orange Sauce (Served with Roast Wild Duck, Widgeon and Teal): Take half a pint of well flavored stock or gravy (free from fat), add the grated rind and juice of a Seville orange (failing Seville oranges use the ordinary sour oranges), a small glass of sherry, and half a saltspoonful of cayenne pepper. Mix these ingredients and put them in a saucepan. Let the sauce simmer for about 10 minutes and serve hot.

Orange Sauce (Another Way): Put 2 tablespoonfuls of red currant jelly into a small basin, and place it in a vessel containing boiling water; when the jelly has melted, add the grated rind and juice of a Seville orange, the juice of half a lemon, half a teaspoonful of salt, half a salt-spoonful of cayenne, and a tablespoonful of port wine. Mix the ingredients well, and serve the sauce hot or cold.

Oporto Sauce: Put into a clean saucepan the following ingredients: a wineglassful of port wine, a dessertspoonful of brandy, and a table-spoonful of red currant jelly, a dozen stoned Morella cherries, a small apple, peeled, cored, and cut up small, and 3 French plums. Boil up slowly and take out the fruit when cooked. Mix a teaspoonful of corn or rice flour and a tea-spoonful of castor sugar with a tablespoonful of port wine; add this to the first liquor, and boil. Pass the fruit through a fine sieve and add to the sauce. Serve it iced or very cold.

Raisin Sauce (Served with Roast or Braised Meat): Stone and wash 2 ounces of raisins, and boil them in a stewpan in half a pint of water for about 20 minutes. Melt in a stewpan an ounce of butter, add an ounce of flour, and stir over the fire until nicely browned, then add half an ounce of sweet almonds, blanched and shredded, the grated rind and juice of half a lemon, a tablespoonful of vinegar, also half an ounce of sugar, a glass of claret, a saltspoonful of salt, and half a saltspoonful of grated nut-meg; then add the stewed raisins, allow the sauce to boil for a few minutes, and serve hot.

Sultana Sauce (Served with Braised or Stewed Hares, Rabbits, and Ragouts): Pick and wash and soak in tepid water 2 ounces of sultanas, and cook them in a stewpan for about 15 minutes in half a pint of water. Mix ½ an ounce of corn-flour with an ounce of butter, and stir it into the boiling fruit and cook until it thickens. Add the grated rind and juice of half a lemon and a small glass of claret. Reheat and serve hot.

Tamarind Sauce (Usually Served with Fish): Mix ¼ lb. of tamarinds with ½ pint of water and rub all through a wire sieve; put the pulp thus obtained into a saucepan, add a wineglass-ful of port wine or claret, the juice of half a lemon, an ounce of sugar, and half a saltspoonful of cayenne. Boil up and stir the ingredients until quite smooth. Add more water, if found too thick. Serve the sauce hot or cold.

Red Wine Raisin Sauce (Served with Roast Beef, Venison or Wild Birds): Stone 4 ozs. of raisins and chop them finely, then simmer in a stewpan with half a pint of Demi-glace sauce for ten minutes, add the juice of a lemon, and the grated rind of a quarter of it, a glass of claret, also a teaspoonful of castor sugar. Boil up and cook for ten minutes, then serve hot or cold.

SWEET SAUCES.

For Hot and Cold Puddings, Fruit Timbales and Croûtes, Fritters, etc.

Almond Sauce: Put into a saucepan half a pint of milk, bring nearly to the boil, then stir in slowly one level dessertspoonful of cornflour or cornstarch previously mixed with a little cold milk; stir till it boils, then add half an ounce of Valencia almonds and four bitter almonds, previously blanched, peeled, chopped and pounded to a paste with 2 ounces of castor sugar; reboil the whole, then add a raw yolk of egg. Re-heat, but do not let it boil again. Serve hot or cold.

Almond Cream Sauce: Blanch and skin one ounce of Jordan almonds and six bitter almonds; then put them in a mortar with 4 ounces of castor sugar and a tabelspoonful of orange-flour water, and pound them finely; remove this and put into a small stewpan, add a gill of cream and 2 egg yolks, and whisk the sauce over boiling water until it resembles a smooth cream.

Almond Sauce for Fruit Salad: Blanch and peel one dozen sweet and four bitter almonds, soak them in cold water for about two hours; drain and chop them, next put them in a little cold water with a few drops of lemon juice, and sufficient salt and pepper to season; by degrees add a few spoonfuls of sherry—just enough to make it the consistency of cream. This dressing may be used on sliced apples, pears, peaches and fresh figs.

Apricot Sauce: Required: 2 tablespoonfuls of apricot marmalade, ½ gill sherry or ¼ gill brandy, 1 gill water, ½ oz. fresh butter.

Put the marmalade in a stewpan, and let dissolve with the water and butter. Remove from the fire, add the sherry or brandy, boil up again, strain, and use as required. A liaison of one dessertspoonful of cornflour added to the above will improve the appearance for cooking purposes. A little sugar may be added if found necessary.

Banana Cream Sauce: Peel three ripe bananas, and rub them through a sieve. Mix an ounce of corn or rice flour with a little cold water into a smooth paste, add to it a gill of cream, stir over the fire until it boils, and allow to simmer for five minutes, then add the banana pulp, about 1½ oz. of castor sugar, and a tablespoonful of rosewater. Re-heat and flavor with a little lemon rind. Last of all stir in a little whipped cream.

Brandy Sauce: Required: 4 oz. loaf sugar, ½ oz. cornflour, ½ gill brandy, ½ pint water.

Put the sugar and rather more than a gill and a half of water in a copper stewpan, boil a few minutes, take off the scum, and reduce to a thin syrup. Mix the cornflour with a little cold water, stir into the boiling syrup, and whisk over the fire for about five minutes. Add the brandy, strain, and serve hot with the pudding.

Brandy Butter: Work to a cream in a basin with a wooden spoon, 6 ounces of fresh butter with 2 ounces of icing sugar, then add by degrees 2 dessertspoonfuls of lemon juice, and 2 to 3 tablespoonfuls of brandy; beat until it resembles whipped cream, and put it on the ice till required. This sauce is good with most steamed or baked puddings; it can also be used as a garnish for cold puddings.

Caramel Sauce: (another way): Put an ounce of loaf sugar into a copper pan and cook it to a light brown color; pour in quickly half a pint of syrup, flavor with vanilla pod or essence and reduce a little. About five minutes before serving incorporate a dessertspoonful of arrow root, previously mixed with a little cold milk or cream. Boil while stirring for a few minutes, then strain and serve.

Chaudeau Sauce: Put into a small stewpan 1 gill of white wine, Chablis, Sauterne or Hock; whisk in 3 yolks of eggs and 1 oz. of castor sugar, and stir or whisk over the fire till the mixture becomes a cream-like froth. It must be hot but not boiling. Pour over the pudding or serve in a sauce boat.

Cherry Sauce: Cream up 2 ounces of fresh butter and 2 ounces of sugar, then add the whisked white of an egg, and about half a pint of cherry pulp, made from fresh or bottled cherries; the fruit should be first stewed. Mix it all well together, and add a tablespoonful of kirsch or rum, and if liked a few drops of liquid carmine. Serve hot or cold.

Chocolate Sauce: Required—4 oz. grated chocolate, 2 oz. icing sugar, ¾ pint of water, 1 oz. fécule or créme de riz, 1 teaspoonful vanilla essence, tablespoonful of brandy.

Put the chocolate sugar, and water in a saucepan; stir over the fire until it boils. Mix the fécule or créme de riz with an extra gill of cold water, add it to the chocolate, bring it again to the boil, and let simmer for five minutes. Pass through a tammy or napkin, return to the saucepan, add the brandy and vanilla essence, and keep hot until required.

Chocolate Sauce (No. 2): Boil half a pint of grated chocolate, add half a gill of cream, stir this on to two yolks of eggs well beaten, return to the stewpan over the fire and stir until it thickens. A little sugar may be added if required.

Chocolate Sauce (Cold): Prepare a custard as follows:—Beat up 4 yolks of eggs, put them in a saucepan with half a pint of boiling milk and one ounce of castor sugar, and stir over the fire until it thickens; do not allow it to boil or it will curdle; add 2 ounces of chocolate previously dissolved and boiled in half a pint of milk. when cool add it to the custard. then pass through a fine sieve; when cold stir in about half a gill of whipped cream and serve.

Claret Sauce: Put in a stewpan 1½ gill of claret with 1 oz. loaf sugar, a piece of cinnamon, and a slice of lemon. Boil up, and add a dessert-spoonful of Brown and Polson's cornflour mixed with a tablespoonful of cold water. Cook for ten minutes, strain and serve.

Coffee Custard Sauce: Put 6 tablespoonfuls of freshly-made strong coffee into a saucepan with ¾ pint of milk and 2 to 3 ounces of loaf sugar; let it boil, strain, then stir or whisk in the yolks of 3 eggs. Re-heat whilst stirring until it thickens, strain, and add a tablespoonful of cream.

Coffee Sauce: Roast 2 ounces of raw coffee berries in a pan over a quick fire till of a chestnut brown color. Then pound them in a mortar. Boil half a pint of water and pour over the coffee. Cover, and let it infuse for some minutes. Now strain and sweeten with plain incorporate a dessertspoonful of arrow root, or cornflour with a small glass of brandy or kirsch. Add this to the coffee. Let simmer five minutes and serve.

Custard Sauce: Beat up two eggs in a basin, and add by degrees a pint of boiling milk. Sweeten with an ounce of castor sugar and stir or whisk over the fire until the mixture begins to thicken and is of a creamlike appearance. Flavor with a few drops of vanilla or lemon essence, then serve hot. Great care must be taken not to let the sauce boil otherwise it will curdle.

Custard Sauce (No. 2): Boil half a pint of milk, beat up two yolks of eggs in a basin, add a heaping tablespoonful of castor sugar, add some flavoring essence if liked, stir the boiling milk gradually on the egg, return into the stewpan and stir over a gentle fire until the custard is formed. It must not on any account be allowed to boil. If liked a little thicker, a teaspoonful of cornflour may be mixed with a little cold milk; this must be added to the hot milk before the yolks, etc., are incorporated. Cinnamon, nutmeg or lemon rind may be used as flavoring in place of essence.

Custard Sauce (No. 3): Put into a bain-marie pan ½ pint of milk, an ounce of castor sugar, and a small piece of whole cinnamon or vanilla pod. Boil for a few minutes, then take out the cinnamon or vanilla pod, and add the yolks of two eggs. Whisk all until it is of a creamy consistency. Before serving add a small glass of sherry or Marsala.

Curaçoa Sauce: Required: 1 oz. fresh butter, ½ oz. flour, 1 gill milk, 1 oz. sugar, 1 whole egg, ½ teaspoonful vanilla essence, ½ oz. finely-chopped pistachios, ½ oz. finely-chopped lemon peel, 1 tablespoonful red curaçoa.

Melt the butter in a small stewpan, stir in the flour and blend over the fire for a few seconds. Moisten slowly with the milk, add the sugar, and stir well over the fire; beat up the egg and add also; strain the sauce into another saucepan, let it get hot, but not boiling; stir in the lemon peel, pistachios, and curaçoa, and serve as directed.

Foam or Whip Sauce: Put into a saucepan the yolks of 3 eggs and one whole egg, 2 ounces of castor sugar, the strained juice of a lemon, a glass of marsolo or sherry and one of brandy, put the pan in a larger one containing boiling water, place it over the fire and whisk until the sauce ingredients resemble foam or broth. Serve hot or pour it over a pudding.

Hard Sauce (No. 2): Cream up 4 ounces of butter with 6 ounces of sugar, then stir in a glass of sherry and the juice of half a lemon. Beat the mixture until a fairly firm cream is obtained. Spread it neatly on a plate and keep on the ice till wanted; serve with hot pudding. Brandy may be used instead of wine.

Jamaica Sauce: Peel two ripe bananas, rub them through a fine sieve, put the pulp into a saucepan with a gill of water, a dessertspoonful of castor sugar, add a tablespoonful of white rum, boil up, and thicken with a teaspoonful of cornflour or cornstarch, previously mixed with a little cold milk. Boil up, add the yolks of 2 eggs, and flavor with a few drops of vanilla essence.

Kirsch Sauce: Proceed the same as directed for brandy sauce, but substitute ½ gill of kirschwasser for the brandy.

Liqueur Sauce: Put the yolks of three or four eggs in a bain-marie pan with a small glass of maraschino, curaçoa or other suitable liqueur, add 2 ounces of loaf sugar previously rasped on the rind of a lemon to extract all the zest and dissolved in half a gill of water. Place the pan in the bain-marie or a large pan of hot water, then whisk the sauce until it has a cream-like texture, and serve at once.

Maraschino Sauce: Take 1 oz. fresh butter, ½ oz. flour, 1 gill milk, 1 oz. sugar, 1 whole egg, ½ teaspoonful vanilla essence, ½ oz. finely chopped pistachios, ½ oz. finely chopped lemon rind, 1 tablespoonful of maraschino.

Melt the butter in a small stewpan, stir in the flour, and blend over the fire for a few seconds. Moisten slowly with the milk, adding the sugar, and stir well over the fire; beat up the egg and add also; strain the sauce into another saucepan, let it get hot, but not boiling; stir in the lemon-peel, pistachios, and the maraschino, and serve as required.

Marmalade Sauce: Required: ½ oz. cornstarch or cornflour, 1 tablespoonful marmalade, ½ oz. castor sugar, the juice of half a lemon, ½ pint water, 1 tablespoonful sherry.

Mix the cornflour with a little cold water in a saucepan, add to this remainder of abovenamed ingredients and place on the fire, stir till it boils and cook for ten minutes, then strain.

Moka Pudding Sauce: Take the yolks of three eggs, one ounce of castor sugar and a liqueur glass of Kirschwasser, a tablespoonful of cream and half a tablespoonful of strong black coffee. Whisk this over a saucepan of boiling water from 10 to 15 minutes, long enough to bind. The sauce is then ready for serving.

Nutmeg Sauce: Boil in a saucepan 1½ gills of milk with ½ ounce of butter and a dessert-spoonful of castor sugar, then thicken with a dessertspoonful of cornflour or cornstarch, add a sufficiency of grated nutmeg to flavor, also a dessertspoonful of brandy, and whisk it over the fire for several minutes. Serve hot.

Orange Sauce (No. 2): Rub the rind of two oranges all over several lumps of loaf sugar, then scrape it off and put it into a small stewpan with the juice and pulp of four oranges, previously rubbed through a fine sieve; to this add a heaped-up dessertspoonful of arrowroot or cornflour, previously mixed with a little cold water, an ounce of castor sugar, and a liqueur glassful of curaçoa. Stir over the fire until the sauce boils, then simmer for about 5 minutes and serve hot.

Punch Syrup: Required: 4 oz. loaf sugar, 1 orange, ½ tablespoonful vanilla essence, ½ gill best rum, ½ gill water.

Rub the sugar on the orange rind to obtain the flavor of half the orange. Put this into a stewpan, add the rum, light it, and cover quickly; let it infuse for a few seconds over the fire, then add the water, vanilla essence, and the piece of orange, and boil for five minutes; strain, and serve hot with the pudding.

NOTE: If preferred, brandy or kirschwasser may be used in place of rum.

Rhubarb and Banana Sauce: Stew 1 bundle of forced rhubarb in a syrup made of 2 ozs. of loaf sugar and ¾ gill of water. When soft, rub through a fine sieve. Cool and add ½ gill of cream and 2 tablespoonsful of banana cut into small dice. Serve cold with stewed rice or with cornflour blanc mange.

Rum Sauce: Boil up in a saucepan ¾ pint of milk with two ounces of loaf sugar, then add a heaped-up dessertspoonful of cornflour or cornstarch previously mixed with a little cold milk, re-boil, and add 2 tablespoonfuls of rum. When serving, mix in if liked a few coarsely chopped peeled pistachio kernels.

Rum Sauce (No. 2): Put into a saucepan ½ pint of water, 3 tablespoonfuls of orange marmalade, and the strained juice of a lemon; let these boil together for five minutes, then strain, and thicken with a dessertspoonful of cornflour or cornstarch, previously mixed with a little cold water, and boil for another five minutes; whisk in an egg yolk, add also a small glass of rum, re-heat without boiling and serve hot.

Raspberry Sauce: Heat up a gill of raspberry pulp or a similar proportion of raspberry jam with 1 oz. of sugar. Mix a tablespoonful of cornflour with milk, cream or water, and stir into the above. Boil for eight minutes, strain, and add rum or brandy to taste.

Sabayon Sauce: Put 3 oz. castor sugar, 3 yolks of eggs, and ¼ gill cream in a stewpan, place it in a bain-marie or vessel of boiling water over the fire, stir with a whisk until frothy, then add 1 gill Maderia wine, whisk it until it begins to thicken and is of light appearance, pour over the pudding and serve.

Sweet Sauce: Put ¾ pint of water into a pan with thinly peeled rind of half a lemon, also of half an orange, 2 ounces of sugar, a piece of cinnamon, and half a bay-leaf; simmer for a few minutes. Mix a dessertspoonful of arrowroot with a little sherry and add this, together with the strained juice of half a lemon and one orange. Stir over the fire until it thickens, strain, and add a tablespoonful of brandy or maraschino, and serve hot.

Sweet Chaud-froid Sauce: Soak ¼ oz. gelatine in cold water, strain and dissolve in a saucepan with 1 gill of cream or milk, reduce a little whilst stirring and add the desired flavoring, such as fruit pulp, vanilla, kirsch, maraschino, or rum. Cook for a few minutes, strain, and add a little whipped cream, stir in the ice till nearly cold, and use for coating fruit: peaches, pears, apricots, apples, etc.

Sweet Lemon Sauce: Put 2 yolks of eggs in a small saucepan, beat up well, and add 2 oz. castor sugar, ½ oz. of cornflour, and the rind of half a lemon chopped finely. Mix thoroughly and work in slowly half a pint of boiling milk. Stir with a whisk over the fire until the sauce acquires the desired consistency, strain, and serve as directed.

Sweet Melted Butter Sauce: Required—1 oz. fresh butter, ½ oz. flour, 1½ gill of milk, 1 dessert-spoonful castor sugar, a few drops of vanilla essence.

Dissolve the butter in a saucepan, add the flour and stir over the fire for a few minutes without allowing the flour to brown; then add by degrees the milk, stir till it boils, add the sugar, and cook for ten minutes. Just before serving add vanilla cream.

Sweet Mousseline Sauce: Required—3 yolks of eggs, 2 whites of eggs, ½ gill cream, 1½ oz. castor sugar, 1 wineglassful maraschino.

Put all the above ingredients into a small stewpan, beat it with a whisk, stand the pan in a bain-marie or a large vessel three parts full of boiling water. Stir until it becomes creamy, but do not allow it to boil. Serve with hot sweet puddings, etc.

Sweet Orange Sauce: Required—2 yolks of eggs, 1 small orange, 2 oz. castor sugar, ¾ pint of milk, 1 glass curacoa.

Boil up the milk and sugar, add the rind of orange finely grated, the tablespoonful of orange juice, stir in the yolks of eggs, beat well over the fire with a small whisk. When the sauce begins to thicken, place in the bain-marie or a vessel containing boiling water, add the liqueur, and continue to whisk for ten minutes; the sauce is then ready for serving.

Cold Strawberry Sauce: Boil up 1 gill of strawberry pulp with 1 oz. of castor or icing sugar. Mix a dessertspoonful of cornflour (or cornstarch) with a tablespoonful of sherry and stir into the above. Cook for ten minutes, strain, add a tablespoonful of cream, and serve.

Hot Strawberry Sauce: Required: The pulp of a dozen large, ripe strawberries, 1 glass of Sauterne or Chablis, 1 egg, 1 oz. sugar.

Put the fruit pulp, wine, and sugar in a small stewpan, whisk over a moderate fire until almost boiling, then add the egg; continue to whisk until quite frothy; on no account allow it to boil. Serve as soon as ready.

Cornflour Sauce: Required: 1 tablespoonful

cornstarch or cornflour, ½ pint milk, 1 pat fresh butter, ½ oz. loaf sugar, lemon rind or vanilla pod.

Boil up the milk with the butter, loaf sugar, and the thin rind of half a lemon or an inch of vanilla pod. Mix the cornflour with a little cold milk in a basin, and pour on it the hot milk, return to the saucepan, boil up, and cook for eight minutes.

Valancia Sauce: Put a tablespoonful of red currant jelly with a gill of water in a saucepan, and stir over the fire until the jelly is dissolved, then add the strained juice of an orange, and some of the rind, finely grated or cut into fine shreds, with a few blanched and shredded almonds or a tablespoonful of desiccated or fresh cocoanut. Sweeten to taste, and serve hot.

Vanilla Sauce: Proceed in the same manner as above directed, omitting the lemon rind and using vanilla pod in its place. A little cream may be added just before serving.

Vanilla Sauce (No. 2): Boil 1 gill of milk with ½ a vanilla pod; cream 3 egg yolks with 1 oz. of castor sugar, and pour over, whilst stirring, the milk. Return all into the stewpan and stir over the fire till it thickens, but must not boil. Strain and serve as required (hot or cold).

Wine Sauce: Put into a jar or bain-marie pan 3 egg yolks, a gill of sherry, Marsala or Madeira, and a tablespoonful of castor sugar. Place the pan in a bain-marie or else in a large saucepan of boiling water, and whisk till frothy and of creamlike consistency. It must not boil or it will curdle.

STORE SAUCES.

Condiment or Relish Sauces for the Kitchen and the Table.

Albany Sauce: Put the yolks of 2 hard-boiled eggs and the yolk of one raw egg, also a little salt and paprika pepper, into a mixing basin, and mix till quite smooth with a wooden spoon, then stir in slowly a gill of Lucca oil, a tablespoonful of mushroom catsup, a tablespoonful of Harvey sauce, a tablespoonful of anchovy essence 2 tablespoonfuls of tomato pulp, and the strained juice of a fresh lemon. Mix all well together, and serve as required for grilled fish or grilled meat (use it as cold meat sauce or as a salad sauce).

Balmoral Sauce: Put into a saucepan a quart of vinegar, 2 ounces of currants, 1 ounce of raisins, a pint of green gooseberries, and 2 ounces of Demerara sugar; let all simmer slowly for half an hour, then put into a bowl a teaspoonful of mustard, a teaspoonful of turmeric, a teaspoonful of mace, and a good pinch of salt; mix together with ½ pint of tarragon vinegar. Pass all through a wire sieve, and mix well together. Put the sauce into bottles well corked, where it will keep for any length of time.

Chutney Catsup: Peel, quarter and core 1 dozen large sour apples, and pass them through a mincing machine, together with 6 tomatoes, 4 peeled and sliced onions, and ½ lb. of stoned raisins. Boil one quart of malt vinegar and one quart of cider vinegar for 10 minutes, with ½ lb. of brown sugar, 2 tablespoonfuls of salt, and a spice bag containing one whole nutmeg, a piece of ginger root, a pounded stick of cinnamon, 12 whole cloves, and a tablespoonful of allspice. Then add the minced vegetables and fruit, and cook all gently to the consistency of a purée. Put it into air tight jars or wide mouthed bottles.

Cucumber Catsup: Peel and grate or chop 2 dozen small ripe cucumbers, put them into a large basin or pan, sprinkle over with salt, and allow them to stand covered for three hours, then pour off the liquid formed. Measure the pulp, and to every quart add 2 peeled and finely chopped Spanish onions, a saltspoonful of cayenne pepper and a teaspoonful each of salt, ground cloves, and allspice. Bring slowly to the boil, pouring in gradually as the catsup begins to simmer a quart of French wine vinegar. Cook for 15 minutes, and when cold pour into bottles or glass jars, cork and seal.

Cumberland Catsup: Put into an earthenware jar 6 lbs, of white or red grapes, place the jar in a larger vessel of boiling water, and cook until the skins of the grapes burst. Strain the juice carefully into a clean cooking vessel, and return to the fire, add to each quart of grape juice ½ lb. of granulated sugar, 1 pint of vinegar, a tablespoonful of salt, a tablesponful of whole cloves, half a grated nutmeg, a teasponful ground allspice, and a tablespoonful ground cinnamon. Boil slowly for about an hour, pour whilst hot into bottle, and cork them well.

Mushroom Catsup: Wipe half a bushel of freshly gathered mushrooms with a damp cloth, and arrange in layers in a large stone jar, sprinkle each layer liberally with fine salt. Let them remain thus for about 12 hours. Mash up the mushrooms well with a potato masher, carefully straining off the juice through a fine sieve or berry press. Add to this liquid a teaspoonful of black pepper, half a dozen whole cloves, and 2 sticks of cinnamon to each pint of mushroom liquor, then boil slowly until reduced about one-half, strain through a muslin bag or cheesecloth, and dilute with 2 tablespoonfuls of spiced vinegar to every pint of catsup. Put into bottles, cork and capsule or seal them.

Tomato Catsup: Take 3 or 4 lbs. of ripe tomatoes and mash them up, to this add 2 large onions peeled and chopped, 4 green peppers also chopped finely, 2 tablespoonfuls of salt, 3 tablespoonfuls of moist or Demerara sugar, ½ gill of tarragon vinegar, 1 tablespoonful of crushed whole cinnamon, 1 dessertspoonful of mustard, and half a grated nutmeg. Put all into a saucepan with 3 quarts of vinegar, boil gently until all the ingredients are thoroughly cooked, which will take about 3 hours, then strain and bottle while hot.

Walnut Catsup: Boil some green walnuts till tender in sufficient water to well cover them, then press them and measure the liquid. To each gallon of this add ¼ lb. anchovies, and 4 oz. shallots, peeled and cut up small, ½ ounce cloves, ½ ounce mace, and 1 clove of garlic bruised or crushed. Boil for about 20 minutes, then strain and bottle and cork.

Dunraven Sauce: Mash up 6 ripe tomatoes and 4 large peeled and cooked apples, and pass them through a wire sieve. Put these into a large jar, and add a tablespoonful of grated horse-radish, a teaspoonful of mustard, a glass of port wine, the juice of 2 lemons, a quart of walnut catsup, an ounce of moist sugar, also a teaspoonful of salt, and ½ teaspoonful of cayenne pepper. Mix these ingredients well together, boil up, skim and strain, then bottle and cork.

Empress Sauce: Peel and chop finely 2 onions, fry them in 2 ounces of clarified butter till of a light brown color, add half a dozen chillies or capricums, cut into small pieces and ½ teaspoonful of salt. Stir all well together for a few minutes, and whilst stirring add the strained juice of a lemon, ½ pint of vinegar, a pint of tomato pulp, a little water, and a tablespoonful of Liebig's Extract of Meat or Marmite Extract. Rub all through a fine sieve, boil up again, then bottle and use as required.

Madras Sauce: Put into a large jar 6 chopped ripe tomatoes, 4 green cooking apples (peeled and chopped), a few sprigs of green tarragon, 2 capsicums, 2 ounces sultanas, 1 ounce stoned raisins, 2 ounces Demerara sugar, and a quart of vinegar. Put the jar in a slow oven for 2 hours. Mix a teaspoonful of mustard, a tablespoonful of grated horse-radish a teaspoonful of ground ginger, and a teaspoonful of salt. Rub the contents of the jar through a fine sieve, add to the other ingredients, boil again and bottle and cork when cold.

Newcastle Sauce: Pound in a mortar an ounce of black peppercorns, and mix with ½ ounce of allspice, a teaspoonful of salt, and a dust of coralline pepper, an ounce of grated horse-radish, and 4 shallots peeled and chopped finely. Put these ingredients into a jar with a pint of good mushroom catsup, together with a pint of Worcester sauce and about half an ounce of bruised ginger. Cover the jar and let it stand for a fortnight, then strain off the sauce and bottle for use.

Onion Sauce: Put into an earthenware jar an ounce of cayenne or a similar quantity of bruised capsicum or red pepper, a pint of small peeled button onions, a tablespoonful of salt, 3 tablespoonfuls of Indian Soy, and ½ gill of mushroom ketchup, then boil up 3 pints of vinegar and pour over the ingredients. Cover the jar and allow it to stand for about a week, shaking it frequently. Boil up the liquid with another half pint of vinegar, and pour it back on to the ingredients in the jar. Allow it to stand for another week, then strain and bottle for use.

Queen Mary Sauce (Sauce Reine-Marie): This is a rich brown sauce made with meat gravy basis, thickened with Espagnole and reduced with a little port wine, then add finely chopped fried shallots, chopped parsley, and a little anchovy essence to flavor.

Salad Dressing: Rub the yolks of 3 hard-boiled eggs through a seive into a basin, add one tablespoonful of Demerara sugar, one tablespoonful of mustard, 2 tablespoonfuls of tarragon and a tablespoonful of chilli vinegar, also a teaspoonful of anchovy sauce. Mix these well together, then add by degrees half a pint of cream (two or three days old if procurable). Should a large quantity be made, this dressing will keep good for one month if kept tightly corked in a cool place.

Salad Dressing: (No. 2): Put the yolks of three fresh eggs into a basin, with half a teaspoonful of salt, a little mignonette pepper, a teaspoonful of French mustard, a pinch of English mustard, and a saltspoonful of castor sugar, mix well, then stir in gradually about half a pint of salad oil, with a tablespoonful of tarragon vinegar and a dessertspoonful of chilli vinegar. Stir or whisk well together until of a creamlike texture, then add a tablespoonful of boiling hot water, and lastly about a gill of cream.

Spanish Salad Dressing: Put into a mixing basin 1 gill of cream, 1 pint of wine vinegar, ½ ounce of castor sugar, ½ teaspoonful of cayenne, 1 dessertspoonful of salt, 1 dessert-spoonful of mustard, and mix all thoroughly. Cream an ounce of butter, adding the yolks of 3 eggs at the same time, then stir in about half a gill of boiling water. Whisk to a froth the whites of 2 eggs, and add this also, then blend both mixtures. Stand the basin in a pan of boiling water, and whisk until the sauce is quite warm, lastly stir in about a gill of Lucca or olive oil. The oil should, however, not be added until the sauce has cooled off a little. Bottle and cork the sauce, and use as required. It is well to always shake the bottle before using the dressing.

Tarragon Cream Sauce: Put into a basin the yolks of 2 eggs, stir well till smooth, and add gradually ½ pint of good salad oil; when creamy add ½ teaspoonful of salt, a teaspoonful of made mustard, and a saltspoonful of pepper, 2 teaspoon-fuls of anchovy essence, a gill of tarragon vine-gar, a gill of thick cream, and 2 tablespoonfuls of castor sugar. Mix well together and bottle the sauce. Shake well before using, as the ingredients settle at the bottom. This sauce is excellent with all kinds of cold meat, or may be used with any kind of salad.

Tarragon Herb Sauce: Rinse in cold water a bunch of tarragon with a little chervil and a small proportion of other sweet herbs, then drain thoroughly on a cloth. Strip off the leaves into an earthenware jar, pour over a quart of boiling vinegar, cover closely and allow to stand for one or two days, then strain, and mix with one-third of Tomato Catsup and one-third of Harvey or Worcestershire sauce. The sauce is then ready for bottling.

Tomato Sauce: Cut 6 pounds of ripe tomatoes into slices, and put them into a saucepan with 2 large onions peeled and sliced, ½ pound of Demerara sugar, an ounce of salt, ½ an ounce of peppercorns, half a teaspoonful of cayenne pepper, half an ounce of ground cloves, and 4 ounces of allspice. Pour over two quarts of vinegar and boil gently for 2 hours. Stir fre-quently to prevent burning, then rub all through a fine sieve. When the sauce is cold, add a little carmine to give it a nice reddish color, then bottle securely and store in a cool, dry place.

Tomato Sauce (No. 2): Wipe the required quantity of ripe tomatoes with a cloth, and bake the fruit in a slow oven until tender. Next rub all through a sieve and measure the pulp thus obtained. To each quart of pulp add a pint of tarragon vinegar, ¼ ounce shallots and 1 clove of garlic, both peeled and bruised, also 1 tablespoonful of anchovy essence. Boil all in a copper pan until the shallots are tender. Now rub all through a sieve again, and re-boil with ½ pint of vinegar and 1 gill of Indian Soy to every quart of tomato pulp.

Tomato Chutnee Sauce: Peel and slice 6 large-sized tomatoes, add to them 4 sour apples peeled and sliced, put into a stewpan with 4 Spanish onions peeled and sliced, a dozen chillies, 6 cloves, a cupful of brown sugar, a quart of vinegar, and boil gently until all is thoroughly cooked. Pass all through a fine sieve; color if liked with a little liquid carmine, then bottle and cork or put into jars, and use when cold.

Universal Sauce (Sauce Universelle): This is a highly spiced cold meat sauce, prepared with a pint of mushroom ketchup, a gill of port wine, 4 peeled and finely chopped shallots, half a pint of vinegar, ground whole spice, mace and cayenne pepper to taste. Mix well and allow to mature before using.

Worcestershire Sauce: Take 3 quarts of strong vinegar, 1 lb. of split raisins, 1 lb. garlic, ¼ lb. eschalot, ½ ounce cayenne, ½ ounce powdered ginger, salt to taste, small bottle of anchovies, and mushroom ketchup. Boil the anchovies, garlic, eschalot, and raisins in a quart of the vinegar in an iron saucepan until it can be pulped through a hair sieve, then boil all together for a few minutes. Bottle when cold. It is essential that the ingredients should be thoroughly boiled before being pulped.

Worcestershire Sauce (No. 2): Put into a mortar ½ ounce capsicums or sweet peppers, ½ ounce peeled shallots and a clove of garlic, and pound till quite smooth. Add a little vinegar and put all into a large jar; boil up one quart of vinegar and pour it over the pounded ingredients, add also a pint of walnut ketchup. Cover the jar and allow it to stand for some weeks, or long enough to extract the flavor of the ingredients used, then strain and bottle for use.

Yankee Sauce: Put into a saucepan 1 quart of vinegar, ½ oz. allspice, ¼ oz. ground cloves, ¼ oz. black pepper, ½ oz. mustard, 2 ozs. ground Jamaica ginger, ¼ oz. salt, ¼ oz. garlic, 2 ozs. sugar, 8 ozs. tamarinds, 1 oz. curry powder, ¼ oz. cayenne pepper, ½ pint sherry.

Mix the ingredients well together, and simmer gently for about an hour, adding enough vinegar from time to time to make up for loss by evaporation. Let stand for a week, then strain and bottle. A little burnt sugar (caramel) or soy may be added to give the sauce a better color.

FLAVORING OR COMPOUND BUTTERS.

Flavoring butters are used for numerous culinary purposes; they were originally introduced for imparting a specially desired flavor to sauces, and for this purpose they are still largely used. They are also very convenient and useful to serve with grilled meat and grilled fish, for sandwiches and toasts. The taste for hors-d'oeuvre and savories has increased considerably during the past few years. Flavoring butters or beurres composés, as they are termed in kitchen French, have been largely introduced in many other preparations besides those above named. They are used under the titles hors-d'oeuvre and savories. They have also proved eminently satisfactory when used for sauces, i. e., "compound sauces."

Flavoring butter is added to sauces at the last moment before being served, the object being to give a sauce the requisite fresh-butter flavor, which is deemed most essential to a well prepared sauce, as it imparts at the same time the appropriate and distinctive aroma of the condiment from which the butter obtains its name. Most cooks are aware that besides the use of these butters for sauces there are many other ways in which they can be employed, for they are eminently suitable for all kinds of sandwiches and for dainty, savory croûtes; the addition of a nicely blended butter makes a wonderful improvement both in appearance and flavor to such dishes. Several of these butters will be found excellent with cold game, cold duck, cold beef or mutton; others may be used for spreading toasts, biscuits, etc. For decorating little cold hors-d'oeuvre and savories these butters are exceedingly useful, as they enhance the appearance of many such dishes.

Take the humble maître d'hôtel butter as an example, and you will have some idea of the many purposes for which flavoring butters can be used.

The following recipes comprise the most popular and most useful flavoring butters. Each one possesses all the essentials of an appetizing, tasty, and well seasoned compound.

Anchovy Butter (Beurre d'Anchois): Ingredients: Six Gorgona anchovies, two ounces and a half of butter, and half a lemon. Method: Soak the anchovies in cold water, drain, take out the bones, wipe dry with a cloth, pound in a mortar with the butter, add the juice of a lemon, rub through a fine sieve, spread on a plate, put on the ice, and use as directed.

Chutney Butter (Beurre à la Madras): Ingredients: Four ounces of Mango chutney, 1 tablespoonful of French mustard, 6 to 8 ounces of fresh butter, and lemon juice. Method: Pound the chutney in a mortar, add the French mustard, and work in the fresh butter, season to taste, and add a few drops of lemon juice. Rub through a hair sieve, place it on the ice, and use as required.

Devilled Butter (Beurre à la Diable): 1½ oz. butter, ½ teaspoonful cayenne pepper, 1 saltspoonful black pepper, curry powder, ground ginger. Mix the butter with the cayenne pepper, black pepper, a pinch of curry powder, and a pinch of ground ginger. Spread on a plate, and use for grilled cutlets, chops, etc.

Mint Butter: Take 1 oz. butter, perfectly fresh (unsalted) and mix with 2 teaspoonfuls of finely chopped green mint, add also a few drops of lemon juice, and blend this well with the butter.

Note: Besides being useful to impart mint flavor to certain sauces, mint butter is delicious for spreading thin slices of bread, when a dainty sandwich made of minced lamb is desired.

Pimiento Butter: Drain a Spanish pimiento, cut it up small, and pound it till smooth in a mortar with 4-6 oz. of fresh butter and a little lemon-juice, then rub through a fine sieve and season to taste.

Horse-Radish Butter (Beurre de Raifort): ½ stick horseradish, 4 oz. butter, 1 teaspoonful chilli vinegar, 1 teaspoonful lemon-juice. Wash the horse-radish, scrape off the outer skin, and grate finely with white part. Mix with the butter, the chilli vinegar, and lemon-juice, and season with pepper and salt. Rub through a fine sieve, spread on a plate, and put on the ice. Cut into diamond shapes or little rounds, and serve with grilled fillets of beef (tournedos) or steaks.

Tomato Butter (Beurre au Tomate): Peel and free from moisture 3 small ripe tomatoes, pound them in a mortar with the same weight of butter, then cook quickly over the fire, season with salt and pepper, and rub through a fine sieve or tammy.

Spanish Butter (Beurre Espagnol): 2 oz. lean ham, 2 tablespoonfuls espagnole sauce, 6 oz. fresh butter, nutmeg. Pound the ham in a mortar till smooth, then add the well reduced espagnole sauce; incorporate by degrees the butter, season to taste with pepper and finely grated nutmeg, and rub through a hair sieve. Keep on the ice till wanted.

Beurre Maître d'Hôtel or Parsley Butter: 1 oz. fresh butter, 1 teaspoonful chopped parsley, 1 saltspoonful of chopped mixed tarragon and chervil, 1 teaspoonful lemon-juice. Mix the butter with the parsley, tarragon, chervil, lemon-juice, a pinch of salt and pepper. Spread on a plate, put on the ice, and shape into pats when quite firm.

Watercress Butter (Beurre de Ruisseau): Ingredients: Watercress, fresh butter, white pepper, and salt. Method: Pick the leaves of the required quantity of watercress, dry them in a cloth, and mince them as fine as possible, then knead them with as much fresh butter as they will take up, adding a very little salt and white pepper. Put the mixture thus obtained on a plate, spread it out evenly, and place on the ice. Stamp out some little rounds and serve in a glass dish, or use for other purposes as described.

Ham Butter (Beurre au Jambon): Ingredients: Four ounces of cooked lean ham, 2 ounces of fresh butter, one tablespoonful of double cream, salt, and cayenne. Method: Pound the finely chopped lean ham, add the butter and double cream; season to taste with white pepper and cayenne. Pass through a fine sieve, put it on the ice, and use as required.

Lobster Butter (Beurre de Homard): Ingredients: Lobster spawn and coral and fresh butter. Method: Procure the eggs (spawn) and coral of a lobster, pound till smooth in a mortar with double its quantity of fresh butter, rub through a fine sieve, and keep in a cool place till required.

Montpellier Butter (Beurre Montpellier): Ingredients: Two ounces of parsley, chervil, tarragon, chives, and cress; 2 anchovies, 9 yolks of hard-boiled eggs, 3 ounces of butter, 1 teaspoonful of capers, and 1 gherkin. Method: Wash and pick the parsley, cress and herbs; blanch for three minutes, strain, and cool. Drain well in a cloth and pound in a mortar. Put this on a plate and clean the mortar. Wipe and bone the anchovies; pound them in a mortar with the egg yolks, capers, and gherkins. When quite smooth add the butter, lastly the green purée. Mix the whole well together. Put through a wire sieve, and use as required.

A little spinach greening may be added if the herbs should not color the butter sufficiently.

Paprika Butter (Beurre au Paprika): Ingredients: Four ounces of fresh butter and 1 teaspoonful of paprika (Hungarian pepper). Method: Put the paprika on a clean plate with the butter, and mix it to a smooth paste, then put it on ice or in a cool place and use when required.

Ravigote, or Green Herb Butter (Beurre Ravigote): Ingredients: 1½ ozs. chervil, 2 ozs. of spinach, 1½ ozs. of green chives, 1 oz. of tarragon, ½ oz. of parsley, 3 or 4 shallots, 6½ ozs. of butter, pepper, and salt. Method: Wash and pick the chervil, spinach, green chives, tarragon, and parsley. Put it in a sauce-pan with water and blanch. Drain well and pound in a mortar. Peel 3 or 4 shallots, chop finely, cook them in a little butter until of a golden color, and put with the herbs; work in 6 ozs. of butter, rub through a fine sieve, add a little pepper and salt and spinach greening if necessary. The butter is then ready for use.

Shrimp or Crayfish Butter (Beurre d'Ecrevisses): Ingredients: ½ pint of picked shrimps or prawns, 3 ozs. of fresh butter, and ½ oz. of anchovy paste. Method: Pound the picked shrimps or prawns in a mortar till smooth, add the fresh butter, and anchovy paste; mix thoroughly and rub through a fine sieve. Keep on the ice till wanted. A little liquid carmine or cochineal may be added to color if found necessary.

INDEX

www.ingramcontent.com/pod-product-compliance
Lightning Source LLC
Chambersburg PA
CBHW011514170626
46810CB00009B/3368